Liam Shea
Visit my blog at https://liamshea.blogspot.com/
And visit me on Facebook, Novelist Liam Shea.

Printed in the United States of America

First Printing: Aug 2019
D and D publication

ISBN: 9781088726570

By Adventure and Mystery Author

LIAM SHEA

Midday's Starless Midnight

Thanks to:
Mary, Joe, Tom, Jesse, Patrick, Bill, Stacy, Mathis, and Jeff.

The people who keep the iron sharp.

CONTENTS

MIDDAY'S STARLESS MIDNIGHT

A Novel
Inspired by Actual Events

By Liam Shea

PREFACE

The Luckiest Man in the World:

It was 1979, The Bee Gees were king of the disco and Harvey Parker, known only as Harvard, had the world on a string. A fine-looking man with a thick crop of auburn hair and green eyes, Harvard could have easily been mistaken for a movie star. If only he had the moral fortitude to go along with his looks, he would have gone far in the world of business. The truth was, and everyone agreed, that Harvard could claim the title of the luckiest man alive. He had always believed it wasn't his striking features, but his luck which set him apart from other people, and he was right. He considered his working for *The Outlaws*, the most criminal motorcycle gang in Texas, his lucky destiny.

His luckiest break was when he and Ruffio Souza's paths crossed. Souza was the leader of the *Texas Chapter of The Outlaws Biker Gang*. He recognized Harvard's potential, and from that day on made him a member of the gang. For Harvard working for the gang meant planning. He had planned dozens of robberies. Not the smash and grab kind, but bank jobs, investment houses, armored car heists, and even a kidnapping. Harvard was not only uniquely gifted with good fortune, but everything he did was golden. Never in his life did anything Harvard organize not go exactly as he intended, which was extremely fortunate for *The Outlaws*. Every time Harvard planned a job, it went smooth and without a hitch.

Even though Harvard worked for the motorcycle gang, he wasn't like the other ratty dressed bikers there. He carried the honorary title of *General* because what he did for the gang was special, and his appearance reflected how different he was from the other gang members. His clean crisp Levi's and plain white t-shirt might seem macho and even rugged to some but they contrasted drastically to the dirty and smelly appearance of the raunchy brutes he ran with. They considered him preppy and soft, even if he was an official *Outlaw*, he didn't quite fit in.

Eventually, after seven years, Harvard felt locked into a situation where his brother gang members ran his life. He had become a kept pet, a token nerd in service to *The Outlaws*, and more specifically to Ruffio Souza. The services he provided for the gang when he started were due to a kinship he felt for his Outlaw brothers; years later he continued, but out of intimidation. Even Souza recognized the change and to keep Harvard happy awarded him the most prized thing he had to offer—position. He granted Harvard a place at his table, and because of it, at that point, Harvard became an official General for the gang.

The gang made his life good, but only because he had never failed them; in his big house, he didn't even live like the other gang members. No, not Harvard, he was special.

*   *   *

Harvard propped his Harley Davidson Electra Glide up on its stand in front of the mansion he called home. He climbed off his hog and headed toward his front door. Out of nowhere, the wind blew a trashy paper onto his boot. It looked like a greasy Dairy Queen wrapper. He shook it, but it wouldn't turn loose. Somehow it awkwardly lodged under the chain which decoratively wrapped over the top and around the heel of his *Harley Davidson* branded boot. He cussed and bent down to remove it. Under the greasy paper was a fifty-dollar bill stuck to the leather. He pulled it free of the chain and stuffed it into his pocket. Things like that always happened to Harvard.

* * *

The Unluckiest Man in the World:

Donald believed his life was jinxed. Embracing the adage, *if it wasn't for bad luck he wouldn't have any luck at all,* he accepted being the most unlucky man alive. Although he wasn't completely unattractive, with a mop of red hair and green eyes. As it was, Donald could pass for sixteen, even though he was much older. He considered his youthful appearance another of his curses.

Life never turned out as he hoped. He thought that somewhere in his past a spell-caster, probably his own mother, hexed him to forever live a vexatious existence. Martha Wiseman, Donald's mother, not only had a controlling presence but on more than one occasion had manipulated his life to suit her.

When Donald was twelve years old, he asked his mother why she was always so grumpy.

She told him, "It's your fault Donald. Yours and your father's. I could have been something special. I could have been a movie star or a politician, if it weren't for you. Years ago I made plans to divorce your father and leave this miserable town... then I learned I was pregnant with you. After that, I couldn't leave. How would I have made it big with you holding onto my dress tail?"

He never told his father what she had said. Although it wasn't long before Frank, Donald's father, decided to get Donald some help, some counseling. Donald was always so nervous and his mother seemed to cause him a tremendous amount of anxiety. Frank sent him to Dr. Author J. Palmer, a psychologist. Maybe he could help Donald with his obvious resentment toward his mother. Donald's psychologist provided the young man with an outlet to vent his frustration. It seemed to help. He and his mother had gained a better footing in their relationship.

The doctor categorized Martha Wiseman as a narcissist, but Frank just called her *one in a million*. Still, Frank knew better than anyone the price it took to live with Martha Wiseman. He called their marriage *a work in progress* long before Donald was born.

Frank knew Martha blamed Donald for, as she put it, messing up her life. She always blamed him for her missed opportunities. Listening to her a person would think she could have been the first female President of the United States, if not for Frank and that baby.

Of course, Donald wasn't a baby anymore. In fact, he had graduated high school, gone to a trade school and became the lead pressman for a very successful printing company. It might have been because of some greater unseen force, or a flaw in the hex preventing Donald's misfortune from passing across the threshold of the *Bobwhite Printing Company*, but for whatever reason Donald didn't have tragic accidents there as he did most places.

When he was young, he kept his friends, the Michaels brothers, around because they annoyed his mother. He did it even though they were bullies and at times completely, and viciously mean to him. His satisfaction, no, his revenge was that he had found a way to spite her. The problem was, no matter how he felt, no matter how she felt, Martha Wiseman was and would always be, Donald's mother.

When Donald fell in love with Margret, and they became engaged it made life complicated. Their engagement sparked an all-out war in the Wiseman house, but Donald stood his ground and the wedding was set for July the sixth, 1979. In only five months, his closest friends who were at best mean and cruel were about to become his family. Although the Michaels brothers were physically adults, and over the age of eighteen, Donald believed they would never grow up. Their criminally juvenile behavior just continued and continued. He believed this too was just another part of his curse, the hex he lived with?

So, even though his mother was his bane, Donald considered Margret Michaels to be his lucky star. He felt sure after they were married his life would change for the better.

Some people say their most unlucky day is on any given Friday the thirteenth. Not so with Donald. Every day held unlucky surprises.

CHAPTER ONE

Roller Burger
March 11th, 1979
El Paso, Texas

Harvard rode his *Electra Glide* up to *Roller Burger,* a local drive-in, where the waitresses were known to glide on roller skates over to the cars, or in Harvard's case, over to one of three tables reserved for walk-up orders. After all, he had arrived on a motorcycle. The radio played the current hit by Rod Stewart. The hoarse rocker belted out *Da Ya Think I'm Sexy* on speakers secured under a corrugated metal awning providing shade for the pedestrian's tables.

A young, gum-chewing, woman wearing a modified waitress uniform with a short skirt and a pair of white roller skates, rolled over to take his order. She took a pose with one of her skates tipped up on its toe-stop. She winked at this handsome motorcycle rider and asked, "Honey, can I get you anything—anything at all?"

Harvard replied, "Well, aren't you just the cutest thing I've seen all day?"

She coyly tilted one shoulder and said, "Honey, you haven't seen anything yet." She took the eraser end of her pencil and drew a line up her thigh.

"My, my, aren't you ever so sweet? The menu here just keeps getting better and better. But, right now, Darling, I have a yearning for a cheeseburger and a Dr Pepper." For a brief moment, she saw in his eyes the glimmer of a rebel child, both wild and willful.

The roller-skating waitress wrote his order on a pad and rolled backward toward the restaurant door, blowing kisses at him as she rolled away. Harvard laughed out loud as she glided through the service doors.

Ten minutes later she rolled back over carrying a tray with a large Dr Pepper, a cheeseburger wrapped in paper and stuffed in a logo stamped stand up cardboard holder, a large order of fries, a sizable helping of onion rings, along with a chocolate malt. Harvard looked quizzically at the tray.

Sliding the order onto the table in front of Harvard, she winked and said, "No charge, Honey. It's on the house." then she rolled away to attend to a horn honking impatient driver she'd neglected from the start. He was only one in a line of cars who she'd made wait till she finished Harvard's order. He opened the paper wrapper from around the cheeseburger, and on the inside of the wrapper found her name and phone number.

CHAPTER TWO

Arnold's Diner
March 11th, 1979
Lubbock, Texas

It was the day after Donald Wiseman asked Margret Michaels to marry him, and he couldn't keep his mind on his Heidelberg printing press. Time pressed on like a rusty cog, barely moving, and with it the hulking machine too; it was printing slower than it ever had. He glanced at the clock every five minutes, but to him, the morning was three months and twenty days longer than it should be. That was exactly how long it would be till the wedding.

When the lunch whistle finally blew at Donald's work, the entire place emptied in a furious mass exodus. Precisely one hour later, the whistle would blow again and management expected every employee to be back at their machine. Donald rushed to Arnold's Diner to grab a quick lunch, as did many of his coworkers. Once there he had the choice of sitting in one of the diner's tight booths or up to the lunch counter. Being alone, as well as, among the group flooding in from his work, he chose to sit at the counter beside whoever happened to be there.

The bleached-blonde waitress working the counter was Betty. Although they had never spoken outside of the diner, he knew her because it was her daily task to serve the multitude of blue-collar workers regularly invading the diner's lunch counter.

She went down the line of customers taking one order after another, tearing the order slip from her pad to hang them on a line stretching across an open window where Arnold, the cook, shoved hot orders onto a shelf waiting for Betty to serve them up. Usually, she could work the entire diner by herself, but during the lunch rush, Betty's daughter, Bernice, worked the booths. Snapping her gum and tapping her order pad with her worn pencil, Betty stood by Donald waiting for his order. "Don't take all day bub, I gotta get everyone back to work on time. What do ya want?"

"Just something fast and easy for me. How about a hot pastrami on rye and a cup of your great coffee?"

"It don't matter to me. If it tickles your fancy then that's what you get." She poured him a cup full of black coffee, scribbled the order and hung it on the line before moving on to the next guy in the row.

Donald sat at the counter drinking his coffee as the other customers, even the ones who ordered after him, finished their burgers and hot plate specials. He watched new customers place their orders and get their food. His lunch hour was running out. He called Betty over and complained,

"I've been here forty minutes, surely it doesn't take that long to fix a pastrami on rye."

"Hold up, bub. No use getting your panties in a bunch," Betty said. "I'm sure it will be out in a bit."

It was Donald's turn to bellow. "I don't have a bit, I have to be back on the floor in fifteen minutes."

She leaned up to the window and yelled, "Arnold, that pastrami on rye ready yet?"

The gruff voice of Arnold screamed back, "What pastrami on rye? You didn't turn in an order for a pastrami."

"Yes, I did. I hung it up here almost an hour ago."

Arnold burst out of the swinging door separating his orderly kitchen from the chaos of the loud lunchtime rush. Donald had never seen him before because the cook had always stayed hidden from the public behind the small window where the meals came out. To Donald's surprise, Arnold was a round little man with gouts of bristly grey body hair bulging out from the top of a dingy wife-beater undershirt which he wore under his cook's apron. "Betty, you lost your mind or something. You didn't turn in an order for any damned pastrami."

"Now look who's got his panties in a bunch. I did too. I hung it on the line with the corned beef and gravy on toast."

"The hell you did. Betty, I'm telling you, you're losing your mind. That hair bleach has finally rotted your brain."

"I am not crazy. I hung it right here only—" She stopped bellowing and suddenly got a sheepish look. "Here it is. It fell between the stainless steel tubs where the flatware is stored."

Arnold turned and bolted back to his grill yelling, "Betty, I told you I didn't get any damned pastrami order."

Turning to Donald she politely said, "Hey bub, I'm sorry about this, but it's no one's fault—truly. It just happened. How about having the coffee on the house and calling it even?"

He had two options, make a scene or be polite and leave. He said, "Don't worry about it, Betty. It's okay," and with that, he left the restaurant—hungry. He got back into his old Ford Pinto only to find it wouldn't start. It was a good thing his father was a mechanic. He called himself a mechanic even though he held an Associate's Degree in Automotive Technology.

Donald, a slave to his own ill-fate, would be late to work again. He went back into the restaurant to make the call. He hoped his boss wouldn't be too mad, but he knew he would— it was just how his life went.

Donald returned to the counter and asked Betty if he could, please, use the phone.

Betty snapped her gum and said, "Sorry bub, the phone is for employees and emergency use only."

Attempting to remain calm Donald replied, "Since you lost my order making me not only late for work but late and hungry. And now, this hungry customer's car won't start, not to mention how awkward it is for you because it's parked straight in front of your door. Pardon my stupid assumptions, but I think this constitutes an emergency."

Arnold hollered from behind the window. "Betty, give the man the damn phone."

She reached under the counter by the cash register and slammed a Southwestern Bell corded desk phone onto the counter. Sourly she told him, "Five minutes, and no long-distance calls," before she returned to serve the herd of workers at her counter.

*   *   *

Frank Wiseman told his son, the battery was shot because of a short in the radio. Leaving the Pinto at the restaurant, he took his son to work. He would have the little Ford towed to his shop where he could put in a new radio and a new battery.

It was a good thing very few people could run a Heidelberg printing press. That was Donald's only job security.

CHAPTER THREE

The Metal Horse Saloon
March 15th, 1979
Tuesday
6:35 PM
El Paso, Texas

Harvard rode his Harley up into the parking lot of his favorite honky-tonk. In 1979 high waisted polyester disco bell-bottom pants and slick rayon printed shirts were the rage, but not for Harvard. He didn't fit into the hip disco crowd, his domain was biker country. He propped up his H.D. Electra Glide in a line with a dozen other Harleys.

This place wasn't for everyone; the holiday riders weren't welcome here. He walked up to the step in front of a black door. Above the door hung a sign with the icon of a hybrid creature, half motorcycle, and half horse. It heralded this to be the Metal Horse Saloon. The door had been unevenly painted with store-bought spray paint. The rest of the building glowed white in the twilight from the bare florescent bulbs in loose chain suspended fixtures hanging on both sides of the door. He knocked. A bouncer slid open a speakeasy vent. Stern eyes under bushy eyebrows gazed out in silence.

"I ride a dark horse," Harvard stated.

The bouncer said nothing before he closed the slide. Then a loud click and Harvard pushed the door open to his favorite biker bar. Inside he passed tattooed men and their women who were easily identifiable as members of *The Outlaws*. Many of them brazenly wore their emblems on the back of their dingy sleeveless jackets.

Across the bar, a burly bearded biker started a heated argument with a muscular woman about the reason he scratched the cue ball during the last round of pool. It ended when she slapped him with the pool stick and racked the balls again. He recovered from the pole whipping, grabbed her up in his arms and kissed her hard on the lips. All forgiven, it was back to playing *Eight Ball*.

A woman wearing nothing but black leather shorts and an Outlaws vest stood in Harvard's way. Without a word she put her arms around his neck and kissed him. It was a long, deep, and passionate kiss. Their lips parted and she hesitated feeling his breath on her lower lip. She looked into his eyes and said, "Looking for a good time tonight, Harvard?"

He returned the stare, looking past her black eyeliner and smoky makeup. "Drink first. Play later." He turned her around and slapped her rump sending her on to someone else.

Harvard pulled himself up to the bar and yelled over the loud rowdy patrons. "Willy, bourbon and water." He could drink all night if he wanted, all of his liquor was on the gang. The bartender placed the drink on a napkin and slid it in front of him. He tasted it. Only the best for their Harvard.

He motioned a *come here* with his index finger calling to Adrian Hernandez, a low-level enforcer for the gang. With the noise level in the bar blaring loud, he felt if Adrian were close then he could talk in low tones and no one else would hear him.

Adrian asked, "Mr. Harvard, you want something?"

"Sit down Adrian. Let's talk about the future." Harvard sipped on his drink as he spoke in half-truths, "You know, I'm always working on one thing or another for the gang, and I've depended on you before to help me dig up facts. Facts are so important when planning a job." Adrian nodded. He had seen the results of Harvard's intricate calculations for himself. He had even reaped some of its financial benefits.

Harvard ran his thumb around the rim of his glass and continued, "I need something unusual and I want you to get it for me." Harvard pressed his finger to his lips, "I'm not ready to tell Souza about it. Let me tell him what it is. You don't want him biting your head off because you mentioned a job that's not planned out yet, and this job won't be ready for a couple of months at least." The truth was he had no intention of telling Souza anything about this plan. It was his and his alone.

Adrian Hernandez replied, "Okay, you got it. What do you need me to get you?"

"I need a list of all the employees at Carlsbad Caverns National Park."

"Is that all?" So far the request didn't set off any alarms. As odd as Harvard thought it sounded Adrian didn't question it. He knew anything Harvard planned usually meant it was detailed and complex. He always prepared for any possible outcome, and Adrian had been asked before to get lists of employees from banks and such. Besides, he had learned a long time ago not to ask too many questions when it came to important men. Still, this request didn't involve a financial institution. It was an inquiry about a National Park. Adrian couldn't guess what Harvard was up to.

"I'm not even sure this idea will pan out. So remember, keep quiet about it."

"Okay. You can depend on me to keep my mouth shut. I'll have the list for you tomorrow night."

"Good man," He turned to the bartender and yelled over the noisy crowd. "Set one of these up for my buddy Adrian."

The bartender hesitantly slid the glass of amber ambrosia in front of Adrian. Top-shelf brands were reserved for the gang's brass, but if Harvard said it was all right, he would do it. The enforcer took one drink and knowing it was the good stuff, gratefully said, "Thanks, Harvard. You know how to treat a brother."

He smiled, promising himself this job would be one for him, not the gang. He toasted Adrian's glass and said, "Here's to Carlsbad. May it reap exactly what I expect."

Adrian toasted him back and splashed the bourbon down his throat.

"I'll get right on those names for you."

"Great. Adrian, you always come through for me."

For the night Harvard put plans for the new private job aside. He turned around on the barstool and looked the place over—focusing on which woman he was going to take home.

CHAPTER FOUR

Margret Michaels Wiseman
July 6th, 1979
Friday
6:30 PM
Lubbock, Texas

Today, Donald and his girl, Miss Margret Michaels, would go to the altar together. When they left the church, they would be known as Mr. and Mrs. Donald Wiseman and the waiting would be over. Margret had made him wait for this day in more than one way, and the anticipation was as hot as the July sun burning brightly in the summer sky.

Inside the church, he began to relax for the first time all day. The air was cool and refreshing compared to the outside where the mercury kept rising to 110 degrees at noon. By 6:00 PM it was still sweltering hot, and the Texas sun would be up for another three hours.

He sat on a back pew listening to the organist practice the song list while the groomsmen, Margret's brothers, slowly gathered. He had history with these guys. His friendship with Harry and Marcus Michaels, the criminally-minded fraternal twins, went all the way back to elementary school. Glen Michaels was the oldest by two years, and Tommy Michaels, the youngest, thought he had to prove himself tougher than the others by acting out in a variety of sociopathic behaviors.

The dilemma of retaining their friendship versus self-preservation often created precarious and sometimes painful situations. It seemed that his engagement to Margret added fuel to their fire. Experience had taught him to be on his guard when these guys were involved. Since they were Margret's brothers, it was mandatory for them to be a part of the wedding.

At the very least, he had the forethought to try and safeguard his car from them by hiding it in a bank's auto garage for the night. It would be safe under the watchful eye of security cameras and a parking attendant until he could retrieve it tomorrow morning.

Marcus and Harry walked to the back of the church. Harry slapped his shoulder and asked, "Donny, Where the hell did you come from?"

Donald replied, "What do you mean? I've been sitting right here."

"No, you ain't. I looked back here a few minutes ago and nobody was here."

Donald stood, posturing the best intimidating stance he had, "Well Harry, I guess you're seeing things because I've been here." He smiled his final response daring him to dispute his claim.

Ignoring Donald's macho attempt which had as much effect on the Michaels brothers as a pufferfish does on a shark, Marcus said, "So, ya nervous? This is it... your last chance to back out and return to your life of sworn bachelorhood."

"No way. I love Margret. There's no way I'm backing out."

"Ha. Wimp. I knew it all the time," Marcus jeered.

Harry howled, "She's got you whipped and collared already."

If they were going to belittle him, he didn't have to stand there and listen to it. He walked out of the chapel, wandering toward the back rooms of the church. He needed to get away from their yapping accusations. Behind him, he could still hear them calling.

"Wussy!"

"If you're a real man, you won't go through with it. They don't call marriage a ball and chain for nothin'."

He needed a place to be alone and get his head together. He could never explain how he felt to those guys. He was looking forward to married life. He was trading his lousy cursed life for a solid gold version. The problem was, curses usually make a last stand before they dissolve into foul-smelling wisps of memory.

More than one person had remarked about how Donald led a cursed life. But more than anything he longed for the curse on his life to break and allow this night to be special.

After some wandering and thinking, he found himself in the educational wing of the church. He randomly chose a room to make his hideout until he was called on. He planned on sitting in the solitude of silence and darkness until he could get his head together. Suddenly, a shrill scream hit him from inside the room. It was Margret.

Regaining her composure, she said, "Donald sweetie, you know, you're not supposed to see me in my dress before the wedding. It's bad luck."

Outside the open door, turning to face the hall he dropped to the floor. "Margret, is that you? I'm sorry. I didn't know you were in there."

"It's okay. You didn't see much. I think I blinded you with that scream."

"Are you sure you want to do this."

"Do what?"

"Marry me... I mean."

"Of course I do. I love you, silly. And, I'm not about to shack up with you like you first asked me to."

"I know. Anyway, I was just teasing you. I didn't think you would."

"What a way to ask a girl to marry you. Saying if I wouldn't be your mistress then you'd *just have to* marry me. Like I had no choice in it."

Donald smiled to himself. "Well, it worked didn't it."

"Yes... yes, it did. And, you're not getting rid of me anytime soon. I'm marrying you today, Mr. Donald Wiseman. Do you hear me?"

"Yes ma'am, my soon to be Mrs. Wiseman. I hear you." He smiled with the knowledge this love wasn't just a one-sided thing. He truly believed love only worked when it went both ways. Like all young men, he had his share of infatuation before, and his heart told him this was the lasting kind. He sighed again. Would he let her down? He definitely didn't want her to see him as a wuss. He had to do whatever it took to keep the meager macho image she had of him from spoiling."

She asked, "Are you nervous?"

"No, not at all," he childishly lied. "Everything's fine. I'm steady as a rock."

"I guess I was asking because I sure am. I don't know how you do it. Nothing fazes you. You're my perpetual optimist."

The organ music drifted to them through the empty halls. With it came Dora Michaels, Margret's mother.

"Donald! What are you doing here? This is no man's land for the next fifteen minutes. Go away."

He stood and dusted off the black ribbon down the side of his tuxedo pants. Margret called out to him, "Sweetheart, I'll see you in the church."

"Yes, you will."

"I said go. Now!" Demanded Mrs. Michaels.

Donald wandered for a bit then found his place at the front of the church with David Harford, his best man, and Margret's brothers.

Standing in line, to Donald's right, were the Michaels brothers, Tommy, Glen, Marcus, and Harry. Donald was sure they had cooked up some devilry for the wedding. Glen poked at Tommy when Margret walked down the aisle. They were smiling like they knew something he didn't, and it made him more nervous than ever. His nervousness translated into awkwardness making him pitch back and forth from one foot to the other giving him the appearance of being an immature adolescent who needed to be excused to the restroom.

For Donald, the ceremony was a blur. He barely heard the laughter when he knelt for the nuptial blessing. The groomsmen's cackling made Donald take notice, but he didn't catch on to the joke.

It wouldn't be till later when he examined his shoes, he would realize he had been the butt of yet another prank. The words *Help Me* were written on the bottom of his shoes in silver marker. They must have written it there the day before, or else they had some magic trick he didn't know about.

At the moment he didn't care. He was walking through a neurotic haze. Nerves and ridicule created pressure in his head, filling his ears with white noise. Then everything suddenly became calm when Margret tossed back her veil and took his hands. He looked into her brown eyes and found himself lost in their depths. Somewhere in the distance, he heard a man saying, "You may kiss your bride." He stood mesmerized until David nudged him and he moved in for the ceremonial kiss.

"Sweetheart, are you ready to blow this pop stand?" Donald asked.

"Absolutely! Let's get the honeymoon started as soon as possible."

"What do you say we run to the back door?"

"After you, Darling."

"No. Let's do this together."

Then the curse started its last stand in Donald's life. It wasn't going to give up without a fight.

The newlyweds turned and together they hand –in – hand rushed down the aisle. That was when Donald stepped on Margaret's gown and they both fell face first onto the carpet. The bridesmaids hurried to help them up while the groomsmen stood by doing nothing and laughed.

CHAPTER FIVE

L&J Cafe
April 14th, 1979
Thursday
12:28 PM
El Paso, A Quarter Mile from I-10

Harvard received the list of employees from Adrian a month ago, but planning the way Harvard did, took time. He sat next to a half-eaten cheeseburger and a Dr Pepper as he went over the list again. There were three names on the list that interested him. They were men who answered to the last names of Loadstar, Hawk, and Thompson. They worked in the subterranean restaurant at Carlsbad Caverns National Park. Since receiving the list he had quietly started a manhunt for those three individuals who he felt were important to his plan.

From his research, he knew they had all been raised on the Jicarilla Apache, Indian Reservation north of Los Alamos. To pull this job off he needed four men, three men who could be tempted with a fast million dollars, and of course, himself calling the shots. It looked like Loadstar was the leader of the trio. Every group, gang, or organization had a leader. It was time they got a new one. He spent every available minute over the past month making profiles for each one of the men and predicting how they would react in a given situation. Before he initiated his plan, he would need a few days to get them ready. They would have to learn to follow his orders and how to fire an automatic weapon. This job would be the most dangerous and daring thing he had ever planned. The thought of it excited him.

Everything hinged on the fact that he needed these exact men, not anyone else would do. They were uniquely qualified in every way for this job. He knew, with them, he could pull it off. He must bide his time and catch them at the right moment. He would approach them at a time when their defenses were down, and they were vulnerable to suggestion. It might take a while, but he couldn't rush it. This first impression would set the stage for the entire caper. If he failed to recruit them at his first introduction, he wouldn't get another chance. The profile told him Loadstar, the most gregarious of the group, was cocky and would have his guard up. If that were the case, then his private job was doomed before it began.

Over the next month, Harvard kept tabs on the men while he tended to important Outlaw business. Finally, he had a break from his Outlaw duties and on June twenty-first he was able to sit back and look at some *new* information Adrian gave him. Suddenly he visualized his final plan. The new intelligence had turned up something interesting. The men were scheduled to go on vacation together the week of Independence Day. He smiled. People on vacation do one thing if nothing else, they spend too much money. These men loved to drink, and nothing eats money like buying booze. It would be the perfect time to recruit them.

He would arrange their meeting to appear to be a serendipitous act of fate. He made plans to be in Abilene the week of Independence Day. That was where Loadstar, Hawk, and Thompson were spending their time off. They would be putty in his hands and when he was through training them, they would kill for him if necessary. He counted on that. There might be some killing if things went sideways. If it was the price of success... then killing it would be. He thought of the unpredictable mass of people involved and whispered the words out loud, "There could be lots of killing."

CHAPTER SIX

The Wedding Night
July 6th, 1979
Friday
9:30 PM
Lubbock, Texas

The night's events were still hurtling by Margret and Donald like a freight train. They were oblivious that the reception line was long and tedious. True to form the young men made rude jokes while the bridesmaids manned the serving tables with devoted care. Soon Margret decided to retire to the bride's room to change into her going-away dress. Donald stayed out front shaking hands with the out-of-town guests, and refereeing when Uncle Terry and Uncle Bob decided it was time to hash out ten years of dirty laundry in front of both families.

After a few more drinks they were dancing with the bridesmaids. It seemed all was forgiven except for their wives, Aunt Lolly and Aunt Hootie, who sat staring at their flirting husbands in disapproval.

Gladius, Dina, and Ralna, three of Margret's bridesmaids, came over to Donald with a paper bag in hand.

Gladius said, "Here Donny. You better take this to Margret. I found it in the trash."

Confused he didn't say a word as he opened the bag. Inside was the silk dress Margret had made as her going-away dress. He said, "Damn it to hell. Can't they give her a break?"

"I cleaned it up as much as I could. I don't think anyone will notice the little stains I couldn't get out." She paused, then said, "You don't have to tell her where I found it. Just say they took it and you got it back." Tears welled up in her eyes. "It would break her heart." She bit her lip. "I saw Tommy stuff something in the garbage bin and I went to see what it was. Good thing too."

"As you say. They took it and I got it back—said and done."

She nodded and the girls returned to the guests.

Donald went to the room reserved for the bride. He found Margret putting her veil into the storage bag and straightening her dress. "I thought I packed my going away dress. I guess I must have left it at home."

"No, you didn't. I rescued it from Tommy." He smiled the most comforting smile he could. "Mrs. Wiseman, you better get dressed, we're gonna blow this pop stand in a few minutes."

She smiled back. "Whatever you say, Mr. Wiseman."

Donald noticed how she frowned at the stains left in the fabric, but she didn't complain. She primped, fluffed and fixed herself as if nothing was wrong. That was when David knocked on the door.

"Donny, are you in there?"

Donald stepped out of the room. "Yeah. What's up?"

David stood outside the hall fighting down the bouffant ruffles on his tux shirt that piled up under his chin. "I hate tux shirts. All these ruffles make me crazy. "

"Is that all?"

"Uh, no. I can't take you to the hotel." Timid determination edged his voice.

"Why not. Dave, you're our ride. You and Jennifer are supposed to whisk us away from here."

"Those friends of yours are threatening to destroy my new car if I take you guys away."

"What? Don't believe a thing they say. They're just blowing smoke."

"No... They mean it. That's a new car I got and I'm not risking it. You'll have to find another ride."

"Where am I going to find another ride at the last minute?"

"I don't know. Ask one of your *friends* to do it. Jennifer and I are leaving. They're your friends, but aren't they also Margret's brothers? Can't she ask them to help?"

"Something tells me they're not in a helpful mood."

David felt Donald's tension and changed the subject to defuse his temperament. "I never asked, but are you two going on a honeymoon?"

"If everything goes as planned, we'll head out tomorrow about noon to Carlsbad, New Mexico."

"Really? Nothing there but sand and a cave."

"That and the Howard Johnson."

"Who needs sightseeing on a honeymoon anyway, right?"

"Margret has her heart set on seeing the caverns. I guess we'll be doing some sightseeing for sure."

"Sounds lame to me, but it's your honeymoon. By the way, Bob and Terry are going at it again."

"Okay. I'm not seriously worried about them. They've been heckling each other for at least ten years. I don't think they'll choose tonight to let it get out of hand."

"Okay then," he said, "Well, we're out of here."

With that, Donald returned to the reception room just in time to see Uncle Terry push Uncle Bob a bit too hard. Uncle Bob crashed forcefully into the groom's table making the chocolate icing with the plastic ball and chain decoration fly one way, and the cake another. This started a shouting match and more shoving.

It was time for the bride and groom to take their leave of the festivities, but since David had bowed out, Donald hadn't decided who to ask to take them. Who could he ask that had the guts to run whatever gauntlet his friends had planned for them? Suddenly, Uncle Bob's pushing turned into short jabs and Donald made an immediate decision. He approached Uncle Bob and asked if he would do the honors.

Bob smiled from ear to ear, suddenly the pushing was forgiven. Everyone was back on track and Bob was going to drive the getaway car.

He pulled up to the outside door of the reception room and waited for the happy couple. No sooner had the car doors shut behind Donny and Margret, when Harry and Marcus ran over to the car pouring baby oil on the windshield followed by a hefty spray of shaving cream. Bob turned on his windshield wipers spraying water on top of the oil. The combination created a gloppy mess. He slowly pulled away from the church with barely a clear spot through which to see the road. He kept the washer blades running constantly. Behind him, a honking line of cars followed. The Michaels gang had recruited ten other guys and they all embraced the idea of an old fashioned *Texas Style Shivaree*. With tin cans hurriedly tied to the back of the car, the chase was on. In reality, it wasn't much of a chase since Bob couldn't see the road well. He never broke thirty miles an hour. The caravan behind had no difficulty following everywhere Uncle Bob went.

Margret asked, "How far are they going to take this?"

He wanted to say, *Don't ask me. They're your brothers. You know them better than I do.* Instead, he replied, "Honey, I don't know," and swallowed hard. "I promise everything will work out fine. Trust me, it's gonna be okay."

Every traffic light meant more oil and foam was doused onto the windshield. After driving for over an hour the needle on Uncle Bob's fuel gauge dropped to the *E* and he pulled into a station for gas. Aunt Lolly had used over three quarters a tank out shopping, leaving only a bit more than a quarter tank when he left the church. He pulled up to a Texaco gas pump while the *Shivaree* caravan waited on the side of the road behind the station's driveway.

The boys sat on the hoods of the cars yelling slanderously vulgar remarks and making obscene jeers at the newlyweds. The station attendant discretely kept a watchful eye on the hecklers as he pumped gas into the car. He started to wash the windows with his leather shammy but stopped when it filled with the oily gunk and made the widows worse, instead of better. While the gas was pumping, Uncle Bob stepped out of the car, put on his work jacket, and walked over to Marcus who was sitting on the lead car. Donny couldn't hear what was said except that Bob opened his coat like it was a bird's wing. Suddenly Marcus threw down his can of shaving foam and threw up his hands. As Bob walked back to the car the caravan dispersed one by one.

Uncle Bob paid the gas station attendant, squeegeed the window clean, and got back into the car. Donald exclaimed, "I'll be damned! What did you say to make them back off like that?"

"I told 'em they had their fun and it was time for 'em to go home. I put up with their shenanigans for a while thinking they would get it out of their system. I'm a good old southern boy who enjoys a prank, and I've done my share, but these guys don't know when to quit. I told 'em the next one who'd get behind me was gonna find it hard to drive tomorrow with a forty-five slug through their radiator."

Margret said, "I guess they believed you. They left."

"Hell yeah, they believed me. I showed them my gun." He patted the revolver he had stuffed in his waistband. "I wasn't kiddin'. I've had enough of this shit."

Margret leaned into Donald and whispered, "I like him. Can we keep him?"

"No, we gotta give him back. Aunt Lolly will never forgive us if we keep him."

Bob looked up in his rearview mirror and replied, "Don't be too sure about that. She might wrap me with a bow and hand me over. Depends on the day, ya know."

After the caravan departed Donny and Margret told Uncle Bob to go to the nearest self-service carwash. Feeling responsible for at least part of his misfortune, they helped him wash the gunk off his car. He told them they had better things to do with their night, but they insisted. He had been their knight armed with a shiny sword, or in this case a gun-metal blue Colt. Once finished with the carwash it was time to head to the Hilton, the most expensive hotel in town.

Donny had already checked in so it was straight to the room. Margret seemed impressed with the abundance of rose petals strewn around the room, but it didn't prolong the fact they both hurriedly discarded their clothes and headed to bed. Donny was in the middle of a series of kisses and planning his next move when Margret tapped him on his shoulder.

Their lips parted and Donald said, "What? That tapping isn't very romantic." It was only then he realized she had a concerned look on her face.

"Listen," She said.

Donny listened for a moment and started kissing again.

"No... stop. Listen. Do you hear it?"

Aggravated, he said, "What? What am I supposed to hear?"

Holding the covers up to her chin, she demanded, "I can hear it... I know you can too. Something's wrong."

For the first time since they were in the room together, he managed to stop and listen. There it was, a definite drip, drip, drip. He said, "Yeah, I hear it."

In his tighty whiteys, he rolled to the far side of the bed and plopped his bare feet onto soggy carpet. In disbelief, he stood peering around a half wall to where a water pipe in the ceiling had burst, spraying the inside of the dead space and soaking the Celotex. As Donald watched, it was sagging and falling from the ceiling. Reluctantly, he asked his new bride to put her clothes back on and gather her things.

Dressed again, he quickly packed up the assortment of things he had arranged. His perfect night had turned into a harrowing test of patience. He zipped everything up in his suitcase, and together they made their way to the front desk.

The hotel night manager apologized saying, "I'm so sorry about that. I can't imagine why it would just suddenly start spewing water."

Donald sighed and whispered under his breath, "I can. It's my damned curse."

"I'm sorry," the manager asked, "Mr. Wiseman, Did you say something?"

"I said I hope Margret didn't leave her purse."

She spoke up saying, "No, I have it, Honey."

"Great," He looked up at Margret. "That you have your purse, I mean."

"I'll have the water turned off to the pipe," said the manager, "and, the maintenance crew will be out first thing in the morning."

Donald wasn't pleased, "This is our wedding night. Aren't you going to give us another room?"

"Well sir, there is only one bridal suite in the hotel." He checked his booking list. "Oh dear, I didn't realize—" stopping short, he looked up. "The west wing is unavailable because of renovations. You know the Hilton likes to keep everything first-rate." Then he bit his lip before he continued, "Every regular room I have is reserved. There's only one vacancy in the entire hotel."

"Okay. So, what's the problem?"

"It's the most expensive suite of rooms we have. It's the presidential suite."

Margret couldn't sit on the sidelines just listening. She said, "Well I think we deserve some special consideration for our inconvenience. Especially considering it's our wedding night." Then she looked over at her new husband and asked, "You did tell him it's our wedding night, didn't you?"

"Yes Dear, I told him."

"Well, I could make *some* special arrangements considering how you have been inconvenienced." He put some figures into his calculator and pulled the handle. Then he made more additions and pulled the handle again. "By applying what you have already paid to the room and giving you a twenty percent discount—"

Margret interrupted, "You mean a fifty percent discount and we don't call the newspaper to come inspect the honeymoon suite tonight."

He cleared his throat and replied, "A thirty percent discount...," He paused to see if Margret was going to disagree. She only smiled. "That makes it only cost you seventy-five dollars more."

Donald handed him a credit card. Which the man took and inserted into his card machine. Then he placed a three-part carbon paper form on top of the card and rolled the bar across the top. Handing the card back to Donald he turned and gave Margret the key. "The room is on the fourth floor, the pool level. The room has private access to the pool and a poolside bistro patio." He paused and smiled for effect. "Now, Mr. Wiseman, I have a few papers for you to sign. Nothing much, just that my company needs verification of the discount I gave you, and why I decided to extend the courtesy to you."

Donald said, "Honey, you go to the room. The bell boy will take the luggage for you, and I'll be right there."

A little kiss on the cheek for Donald, and off she went following the bell boy who had their minuscule amount of luggage on a rolling cart.

Donald signed the papers and headed to the room. He tried to look at the bright side... *Maybe all this is a good thing if we get a better room out of it? It certainly is more expensive per night and we are getting a discount.*

He had stepped off the elevator onto the pool level when he heard a scream. It could have been Margret. He hurried on to the presidential suite to find the bell boy wide-eyed standing outside the room and Margret kneeling on the bed, tears raining down her cheeks.

Donald, surprised and confused, asked, "What's wrong?" Then he glanced over the room. Suddenly it hit him. The floor was all but covered with dead cockroaches.

He yelled, "What the hell... you just wait. I'll give them a piece of my mind," He looked for the bell boy who had just moments ago been outside the door, but he was nowhere to be seen. In a rage, he stormed back to the front desk.

After regaling the night manager with a variety of expletive packed descriptions of what he thought of his expensive hotel, he asked him to follow him back to the room.

The manager explained, "The janitorial staff isn't on duty at this hour, so I'll have to clean it myself."

In the meantime, the bellboy made an appearance holding a broom and a dustpan. While the manager swept up the thirty or so dead bugs from the carpet, the boy disappeared again, this time to retrieve the vacuum cleaner.

The manager repeatedly apologized as he explained, "The entire hotel has recently been exterminated and this room, as expensive as it is, evidently, wasn't cleaned after the extermination. Probably because it rarely gets booked. I was unaware of the mess." Talking exceptionally loud, to be heard over the noisy vacuum cleaner as he vacuumed the dressing area between the bedroom and the bathroom, he continued, "Every room in the hotel was just this bad before the cleaning crew tidied up."

He looked up to see the disappointment in their faces. "I tell you what. You're welcome to have your money back if you want to leave, but there are no other rooms available. This is the last one, and I'm already giving it to you at a discounted rate."

Donny sat in the oversized presidential chair and shook his head.

"Margret, what are we supposed to do now? We don't have a car until tomorrow morning. This is the only room they have. What do you want to do?" He checked again to see if by some chance money had magically appeared in his wallet, but it was as empty as before. He had spent every penny of his cash on those rose petals, and cabbies didn't take credit cards in 1979. He turned to the manager and asked, "Is there a hotel shuttle that can take us to our apartment?"

The manager's cordial manner seemed plastic and cold as he said, "Not at this time of night. The driver isn't back on duty till 7:30 tomorrow morning."

Donald said, "We could call on family to help out. Mom," he shuddered, "and Dad could take us to our apartment." His thoughts were: *Of course, it would be just one more thing to live down.*

Margret's eyes were dark with fatigue, but a stubborn resolve made her sit up and stop crying. "Absolutely not. If we can't call on my family, we aren't calling on your family either. I'll make do." Then with less earnestness, she added, "I don't think we have any choice. We're not walking at this time of night. Especially hauling our luggage with us, and I'm so very tired. We'll have to stay here." Donald's introverted frustration was almost at its boiling point. In an effort to console him, she conceded, "It looks okay, now." She tilted her head back as if gravity would hold the tears at bay and deeply sighed. "Anyway, like I said, I'm just too exhausted to worry about it."

Donald blurted out, "I'm so sorry."

"It's not your fault. How were you to know? You didn't plan on the pipe bursting, and bugs being all over the place. This is the Hilton after all. It's supposed to be the nicest place in town."

"I'm still sorry." Silently he blamed his curse for their misfortunes.

The manager hurried the bellboy out of the room and said, "We're done here. If that's everything, we'll let you folks get some rest." He left and closed the door behind him.

It had been a long horrible day, perhaps the worst day of Margret's life. Certainly more traumatic and trying than anyone had a right to ask of a bride on her wedding day. As she relaxed, she started a mental tally of the evening's drama, causing her to relive the dreadful events. It was all too much, too overwhelming, and the tears began again.

Sobbing until she couldn't cry anymore, she laid on the bedspread fully clothed and totally spent. Feeling helpless and unable to make anything better, Donny snuggled up behind her and put his arms around her. Fully dressed, the ill-fated lovers fell asleep.

CHAPTER SEVEN

Old Abilene Town
July 6th, 1979
Friday
9:17 PM
Abilene, Texas

Harvard had tracked down the men he needed for his criminal masterpiece. He stalked them for days, watching as they partied at a different bar every night and pulled the same scam on each unsuspecting bartender. Tonight the drinking establishment of choice was Brenden's Bar and Grill at the end of the strip called Old Abilene Town. He was surer than ever these were the men he needed for his masterplan— the gem in his portfolio of crime.

Soon he would find the right moment to approach the trio, but tonight wasn't the night. He would let them spend more money before he stepped in. Tossing his drink back in one gulp he finished and left a hefty tip for the bartender. He wasn't drunk, not even close, when he left Brenden's Bar and Grill. Loadstar, Hawk, and Thompson had just started partying. They had picked up a couple of flashy of girls who frequented the strip of clubs. The bartender told him, the girls were named Cherry and Peaches, and had a reputation for flirting to get free drinks. Harvard laughed, with Cherry and Peaches around the trio wasn't going anywhere soon, at least they weren't going anywhere he couldn't find them.

In his pursuit of the right henchmen, Harvard had spent the last five evenings in one bar after another along a strip of western-style buildings on the outskirts of Abilene. Their isolated location made it the perfect place to party and get drunk. It was also the perfect place for local hoodlums to mug unsuspecting inebriated tourists trying to have a good time. As he left the bar two men, who were sitting on the hood of a car, parked in the bar's parking lot, followed him.

Harvard took one glance and knew by their demeanor they were rank amateurs. Both looked like every other disco dude he'd ever met, satin shirts and tight high waisted bell-bottom pants. They were ordinary, one having mousey brown hair and his friend being bleached blond. It was the purple fringed vest the bleached blond wore which stood out like a beacon. Any experienced criminal would have tried to look more inconspicuous.

He turned, walking between two bars. The alleyway was dark and littered with trash, perhaps by careless waiters in a hurry to dump the garbage and leave work. Harvard moved into a shadow. He stopped and waited. As he had predicted, the two men followed him, expecting to find a drunk or at the very least an easy mark. Harvard stepped behind the men as they unwittingly passed his shadowy niche.

He called to them, "Boys, you lost?"

They turned, startled by his sudden appearance. The bleached-blond answered, "Hey man. How's it hanging? Did you have a groovy time in the bar? Find some company?"

Mousey brown pouted and asked, "Did a girl named Peaches flirt with you in the bar?"

They all but giggled like school girls. Bleached-blond said, "Only when it came to leaving with you, Peaches split. She didn't want your action, only your cash."

Mousey brown added, "Man, she was juicing you for the drinks, sucker."

The other one laughed and added, "I think he saw us coming and wanted us to give him a good time." They snickered, laughing at their own joke.

Harvard clasped his fist hard; they had put him in a bad mood. He said. "If you call getting an ass whipping a good time, you're in the right place."

He unclipped the chain he wore on his billfold. It was lightweight, a perfect weapon. Even though he hadn't been allowed to personally join in the gang's larceny he had done his share of fighting. He had been up against bigger and meaner men than these Travolta wannabes.

The disco dandies suddenly had second thoughts about their chances of mugging him. It was obvious he wasn't drunk and he didn't act like an easy mark. The amateur thugs thought maybe they had bit off more than they could chew.

Harvard started swinging his chain back and forth. "Anytime you're ready we can start this dance. The last guy I hit with this chain lost an eye." He slapped the chain against his wrist, it spun onto his arm like a bracelet leaving a length for Harvard to pop in front of him like a garrote.

The wide-eyed dandies glanced at each other. Harvard could almost see the terror turning the whites of their eyes to a piss yellow. Like a shadowy demon, he backed them up against the brick wall. In a panic, they tried to run past him, but he managed to grab the purple vest and slam bleached blond back into his fist. Blood burst from his nose spraying the purple with red splatters. The dandy yelped and ran after his friend. He wouldn't be seeing them again anytime soon. The fun was over too fast. It left Harvard with the quickening desire to hit something, or someone.

He walked across the gravel parking lot to his motorcycle and looked down at the wheel. A paper had blown into his spokes. It hung there beckoning for him to remove it. He reached down and pulled free a twenty-dollar bill. Things like that all ways happened to Harvard. Without a second thought, he stuffed the money into his shirt pocket and sighed, regretting they weren't up for the fight. Harvard straddled his motorcycle and rode to his hotel. Not much to do in Abilene after 9:00 PM except get drunk, and he needed to keep a level head. He was too close to setting up the critical part of the plan.

CHAPTER EIGHT

Kathrin Souza
July 7th, 1979
Saturday
9:17 AM
El Paso, Texas

Ruffio Souza sat at the table he called his office in the Metal Horse Saloon. Across the table sat Adrian Hernandez. He was nervous and had good reason to feel worried.

Souza's *migas y patatas bravas* sat untouched in front of him. The cook at the Metal Horse always catered to Souza's tastes. Ruffio said, "Harvard has disappeared. He's split, left town without telling anyone. Man, that's not cool." He took a bite of the papas and washed it down with his *Dos Equis*. "Hey, Adrian. Man, Willy, the bartender, says you're a fucker. Is he right, Adrian? Have you been fucking with *The Outlaws*? Said you and Harvard's been talking quiet, all hush, hush. Says he couldn't hear what's been said cause ya'll are always talkin' low and secret like. So, *Chico*, I want to know why you and Harvard are keeping some hot-damn secret from the gang. Like, shit man, there can be no secrets from the gang. A brother like you should know that." He took another bite of his breakfast and stared at Adrian. Chewing in silence, he waited for Adrian to say something. These would be the most important words the enforcer ever said.

Adrian looked around the bar. At every door stood an enforcer, Souza was expecting trouble. Adrian didn't understand. "Boss, I only did what Harvard asked me to. He said he needed some research shit to finish planning a job. It was all for the gang. I promise it was all gang business."

Souza smiled and forked more of his eggs. His eyes weren't reassuring, and his voice didn't sound sincere as he leaned toward Adrian trying to talk brother to brother. "Hey, what the hell man, you got a guilty conscious? You're not in any damned trouble. I know you'd never fuck with *The Outlaws*. You only do what my generals tell you to. I'm not suggesting you're plotting against us. If you were, I'm sure you would have made contact with some branch of law enforcement by now, and you haven't. I know cause after Willie put me onto you, I had you followed. No, you're clean. I just need to know what you and Harvard's been cookin' up. So, tell me, man. I need to know."

"He had me get a list of employees for him."

"So, that son of a bitch *is* planning a new mark. Man, ya gotta like his style. He knows every fuckin' thing about everybody in the bank. Nothin' goes down the man hasn't expected. He plans for every possible situation. It's why he's so good at what he does. Tell me, *chico*, what's he planning? Where is the big hit this time?"

"I don't know?"

Souza put his fork down by the side of his half-eaten breakfast plate. Wiping his mouth with his napkin, he stared at Adrian. "Now, you wouldn't be spreading shit, would you? You know I don't like liars."

"I ain't shittin' ya. I don't know his mark."

"You expect me to believe a little cunt faced son of a bitch like you, don't know? After all those hush, hush talks you've had, and you say I don't know, like I'm just going to take you at your word. You've already told me you got information for him."

"But Mr. Souza, sir, I don't know anything."

Souza started popping his knuckles. "Okay, *estupido*, let's start with what mark you researched for Harvard?" Souza smiled his gold tooth showed a bit more than usual. "The only reason I can figure you'd have to keep a cunt-faced bitch boy like you from talking is that you and Harvard are planning a side job. Are you?"

"No. No, boss. I just don't know what he's planning. He had me find a list of employees at Carlsbad Caverns National Park. He wanted to know who was on staff at the park."

Souza looked puzzled. "Really, man, you expect me to believe he wanted names of people who work for the National Park Service? Not likely." He picked up his fork and started pushing his *migas* around the plate. "It's far more likely you and he are planning to split a take separate from the gang." He pronged a fork full of migas and said, "I can find out for myself, but I'd rather you tell me the truth. You know how stupid lying makes you sound? Man, you don't want to look stupid, do you? Adrian, are you a stupid *chico*?"

"No, Boss, No."

"Bad things happen to stupid people. Stupid *chicos* end up being bitch boys for Hector." Souza pointed over toward his personal enforcer, Hector Vega, a Mexican built like a ton of bricks and covered with prison tattoos.

Adrian watched Hector from across the room as the enforcer put on his brass knuckles and smiled.

"Hey, Hector. You wanna fuck with a cunt faced bitch boy this morning?"

The big man grunted and grinned as he ground his fist onto the palm of his other hand.

Adrian started sweating. Even his cheeks and temples were perspiring. "Boss, it's the honest to God truth. I wouldn't lie to you."

"Okay, Adrian. If you say so then, man, it must have happened just that way." He motioned with his head, and the enforcer by the bar walked up behind Adrian. He took a leather blackjack, from his back pocket, and slapped the consciousness out of the back of Adrian's head. He went limp and fell face first against the table's edge, busting his nose and bleeding down the table leg.

The enforcer asked, "Boss, what do you want me to do with this piece of shit?"

Souza kept forking and eating his eggs. He picked up the spoon and wiped off a dab of blood which had been sprayed across the table when Adrian fell. "Take him out back. He's your shit-eating bitch for now, but don't kill him.

I want to talk to him again. Ya gotta do this right, strip him down, humiliate him, break his self-respect into pieces. Then bring him back to me. By then he'll be ready to tell me the truth. After that we'll make a real example of him, it'll be something to remind every vato and their mothers what happens when someone, anyone, lies to Ruffio Souza."

Souza sat eating breakfast until they returned. Following his instruction, Hector brought Adrian back. Harvard's bloody faced enforcer was only wearing his boxers and had big dark red bruises already showing along his ribs, solar plexus, and his legs. A couple of enforcers propped the semiconscious man up into the chair across from Souza.

Ruffio pushed his plate to the side and asked, "So, vato, you changed your fuckin' story? What big job is Harvard planning?"

In a whisper, Adrian replied, "Boss, I'd never lie to you. He wanted the list from the National Park."

Another toss of his head and Adrian was being dragged out back of the bar again. This time by two different enforcers. Souza called Hector back to his table. "Bro, get my sister. I need to know what Harvard's angle is, and she's the best tracker we have. She'll find that son of a bitch, Harvard, and bring him back. No question about it."

By the time Ruffio Souza finished his second *Dos Equis* Kathrin Souza was pushing open the heavy door to the bar. Wrapped in black, side laced, leather pants and a black leather halter top, she had a dangerously intimidating presence all her own. She might as well have been wearing a danger zone sign across her buxom chest. She was intentionally provocative enough to make any man nervous.

She stood admiring herself in the mirror behind the bar. Leaning closer to her reflection, she used her finger to straighten her lipstick. Ruffio could wait for her. He wasn't going anywhere.

Running her fingers through her hair, she primped and smiled at her own reflection. It wasn't by accident she was known as *The Biker Bitch of The Outlaws.* When she had sufficiently finished admiring herself, she walked across the room to Ruffio's table. She kicked Adrian's bloody chair out of her way and pulled up another. She sat with the back in front, straddling the chair like a man. She inspected the bloody table, and remarked, "Looks like you've already started your morning with fun and games. I'm disappointed you didn't invite me to the party."

He would never talk to her like she was just one of the gang. She was his sister and deserved respect.

"My dear sister, Kat, I would have but I wanted the damned vato to live. You have a nasty habit of taking interrogation a bit too far." He propped himself up on his elbows. "I want you to do something else, much more *importante.*"

"Is that so brother, what do you have in mind? I bet it's not nearly as much fun."

"I want you to find Harvard. Damned genius isn't anywhere he usually hangs out at, and man, I have a bad feeling about his disappearance."

"What? Your gangster wannabe jumped ship? He knows too much about the gang to be going solo." Accusingly she said, "*Hermano*, you have made him a very dangerous man."

"Find the son of a bitch, and bring him to me." He smiled showing his gold tooth. "Like man, I don't want him killed, understand? I want him back where he belongs doing what he does best. So, *hermana*, find him for me."

She stood and flexed her lean muscles like a cat after a nap. "Can I have him after you're finished with him?"

"It might be a while, Sis. He has more work to do."

"I'm a patient kitty. I'll be gentle, I promise," she purred.

CHAPTER NINE

Recruitment Night
July 7th, 1979
Saturday Night
8:45 PM
Abilene, Texas

Harvard sat on a barstool at an establishment called Mary's Bar. It was on the outskirts of what the locals called Old Abilene Town. Sitting there in silence while he blew smoke rings listening to the bar-hopping regulars get loud, and boast about their negligible successes. Harvard wasn't the boasting kind. He waited and watched, like the secret weapon he was.

He was about to set up the biggest caper of his career. He'd been working on it for a long time, and finally, it was what he called *recruitment night*. He had stalked these three employees of Carlsbad National Park for weeks and tonight they would become his men—his personal gang. They would be the key to everything. These three unwitting souls were perfect.

At a far corner table sat the three drunk men, hooting and having a good time as they entertained four ladies. They were burning through the drinks quickly and building a substantial bar tab.

Harvard leaned over the bar toward the bartender, and asked, "What's the deal with those guys in the corner. They don't exactly look like your everyday Mexicans." He wasn't making small talk. Manipulation was one of Harvard's skills.

The bartender answered, "I don't rightly know about them. They left a credit card with me to start a tab and they've been partying like there's no tomorrow."

"Do you know their names? Surely you didn't start a tab for them without even getting their names."

"The one on the right is named Mika Loadstar. The one in the middle sitting between the blonde and the redhead is named Hinto Hawk. It's his card I'm holding. The guy on this side of the strawberry blonde is Tarby Thompson. The girls are regulars. I see them in here every week. Peaches, Cherry, Brandy, and some other slut, I think they're working girls... if you know what I mean. It's for sure, they're working those guys."

"Really, is that their names, Loadstar, Hawk, and Thompson, huh?" He smiled at his clever ruse. He knew these guys better than their own mothers and it was time to reel them in. By this time, in their vacation, they should have run out of money. That credit card was probably worthless, and he doubted they even had enough for gas to get back to Carlsbad. Harvard smiled and asked, "Are you going to let them drink all night?" He folded a ten and put it under his glass for a tip. "Don't you think it's time to collect on their tab?"

"You're right. I got busy and let them go too long. I guess I better tell them how much they owe. Looks like their entire tab comes up to three hundred and ten dollars. What do you bet they're at least a hundred in the hole?" The bartender ran the card for the total bar tab. shook his head and sighed. "They'll end up washing dishes all next week for what they owe." He took a pair of scissors and cut the card in two.

"No, they won't. I'll see to it, but for now, you go collect and see what they say."

As soon as the bartender tossed both halves of the credit card on the table, and the girls split, not wanting to ruin their French tips by washing dishes. All their flirting was a sham to get free drinks, and they didn't want to be held responsible for any part of the tab. The guys made all kinds of excuses, but the bottom line was, even after pooling all their cash they were still two hundred in the hole.

That's when Harvard slid into the booth. "Let me introduce myself, I'm Ha—"

"I don't care who you are," replied Hinto Hawk, in a drunken rant. "I'm free like the fucking wind. Nobody can fly high like Hinto." Snickering the words through an inebriated laugh before he threw back his head and guffawed. Black hair and a ruddy brown tan, he was made-to-order for the part Harvard had planned for him.

Harvard paid their delinquent bar tab and said, "Boys, you owe me. As of right now, I own your asses. Bartender, bring us some black coffee... these men have some sobering up to do."

Mika Loadstar, tall, thin, and just as ruddy tan as Hinto, blurted out, "Hell no. I ain't planning on sobering up. That's why I just gave that bartending son of a bitch all my money. I'm drunk and I'm gonna enjoy every fucking moment of it. And, who the hell are you anyway?"

"My name is Harvard. That's all I go by, just Harvard."

Tarby Thompson, a stout, blue-eyed Indian who was barely more sober than his friends exclaimed, "Holy hell! Guys, shut up. Do you know who this is?"

Hinto mocked, "Don't tell me... he's Colonel Sanders."

Mika laughed, "He can't be Colonel Sanders cause he ain't got grey hair."

Tarby slammed his beer bottle on the table, spilling it everywhere. "Get those shitfaced grins off your mugs. This guy is a honcho for *The Outlaws*... you know, the motorcycle gang."

Mika leaned over to Tarby and asked, "Are you shitting me? This gringo is some serious somebody?"

Tarby said, "If he is who he says he is, then yeah... He's a somebody. I had a friend who used to run with that gang. He would laugh and say they had a secret weapon, called it *The Harvard*. I know it sounds crazy because their secret weapon was a guy – this guy."

Harvard leaned closer, "You can wash dishes or sober up and listen to what I have to say." He leaned back and puffed on his cigar. "It's as simple as that."

Mika blurted, "If listening's all we have to do for you to pay us out of debt then talk, Gringo talk." He laughed at the sound of the words and repeated them over again snickering as he said them. "Grrringo talk, talk gringggo, talk."

Harvard was patient as he poured an entire pot of black coffee, one cup at a time, into his new gang. Finally, he thought they were sobering up, at least a little.

"Can you gentlemen be in Carlsbad tomorrow night?" Harvard asked.

Hinto slurred his reply, "Sure we can." He belched and recanted. "Nope, we can't. I mean we could, if we had any money to get there. We're from Carlsbad and work at the caverns, but we're busted—flat broke."

"Imagine that," Harvard smoothly said. "How lucky for me to have run into you guys. You know I could loan you a little something to get you back to Carlsbad."

"Yeah, Gringo. You'd do that for us? You're a fucking good gringo." He snickered as he repeated, "Grrringo, Grinngo. You know who you are."

Harvard handsomely tipped the bartender and had him bring another pot of freshly brewed black coffee to the table. Harvard poured them cup after cup until they stopped slurring their words. When he thought they were sober enough to remember his offer, Harvard said, "If you guys are interested in the prospect of becoming instant millionaires, meet me in Carlsbad tomorrow night at the Indian Nation gaming room. If you're there, I expect you're up to this plan. Right now is the time to decide if you're man enough. If you're not... If you don't have the *cojones* to get a million dollars, then this is the end of our short-lived friendship. You go your way, flat broke, and I'll go mine— with my millions." He left enough money for them to get home, and left strict instructions with the bartender to not keep serving them drinks, only coffee.

CHAPTER TEN

The Apartment
July 7th, 1979
Saturday
11:30 AM
Lubbock, Texas

The next morning Donald and Margret awoke to a loud mechanical roar— the sound of machines cleaning the indoor swimming pool.

"Good morning, Mr. Wiseman," said Margret.

Donald replied, "Good morning, Mrs. Wiseman. What time is it?"

"We've slept the morning away. We were so tired after all the hoopla last night."

"What? Is it noon?"

"Almost, why?"

"I've got to get the car before noon or else it'll be locked in the parking garage till Monday."

"You better hurry. It's eleven-forty now."

Waiting for a shuttle would have taken too long, so Donald flew out the door and hurriedly walked the four blocks over to where the car was parked. As he approached the multi-level garage, he saw a car from a security company pulling away. Angry thoughts filled Donald's mind. *What is he doing? He can't leave. He can't lock my car up!*

He waved his hands and ran the last half block only to find the parking garage had already closed. *I'll be damned. Of all the luck, this damned curse is going to be the end of me yet. This can't be happening, not today. What am I going to do?*

He sat on the curb outside the caged gate. *If I tell Margret what happened it's just another thing added to the horrible night we had. She's going to wonder why she married me after all.*

He grimaced. *How do I say it? Oh, by the way, Darling, we can't go on our honeymoon. She'll say, what? What did you do to make him close early? And, I'll say, No Dear, it's not my fault. The attendant had closed by the time I got there. Then she'll say, you could have made it on time if you weren't so lazy. Then I'll say, no it's not my fault. I don't know why he locked up five minutes early. He probably had plans of his own for the weekend.*

Donald's thoughts were irrational—fearful of disappointing Margret. He was so accustomed to his mother blaming him for everything; he had started transferring those thoughts to his new bride.

She's not like that. She won't throw this back in my face. I can depend on Margret. Then he looked up through the metal mesh encasing the entrance to the parking garage. He could see his car. It was only thirty feet away, but there was nothing to do about it. Until Monday it would be sitting right there, secure from his devious friends, and him.

He muttered and cursed all banks that closed at noon on Saturday. With his self-esteem already shattered, despair started to erode his cheery shield of optimism. Oddly swearing at the situation seemed to help his spirits. The more he walked and cussed, the better he felt. By the time he reached the hotel, he was again his patient, cheerful self.

Margret smiled and greeted him with, "I've packed everything and I'm ready to go. You can take the luggage to the car anytime. I can't wait to get to our new apartment."

It was time to confess. Would she blame him for this new misfortune? He held his breath for a moment before he said the words, "I didn't get the car."

Her hands magnetically went to her hips. "What do you mean you didn't get the car? We've got to have the car. How are we going on our honeymoon? We only have through Wednesday, then you have to be back at work."

"I have an idea, but, first things first. I think this hotel has a shuttle van that takes guests to the airport. I'll see if they can take us to our apartment." With that, he left for the service desk again while Margret waited in the room with the bags. After checking her nails four times and looking at her watch every thirty seconds, she finally took a deep breath and tried to put her troubles behind her. Which would have been easier if new ones didn't keep popping up.

What's taking so long? Maybe, the driver called in sick and there's no one to drive us to the apartment. Maybe, Donald found some money and is calling a taxi? She gasped and suddenly looked stunned as she thought. *Maybe, He met a rich blonde in the lobby and they're going to Carlsbad without me. She shook her head. Nope, he loves me.* She was just venting her frustration. Putting that disappointment behind her she tried to be optimistic. *Maybe things will work out. Donald says everything will be alright in the end. I just have to have faith in my Donald.*

He returned with a smile. "My lady, your carriage awaits." He took her hand as if he were a knight at court and she, a lady-in-waiting.

She said, "Thank you, kind sir. Lead on."

Donald gathered the small amount of luggage they had with them, and they waited at the front of the hotel for the shuttle van. He confessed, "Last night didn't turn out exactly as I planned it, you know."

Margret smiled and caressed his cheek with a tender touch. "I know. At least it will be a night to remember." She tilted her head back and forth briefly before continuing. "Maybe they aren't the memories I was expecting, but believe me, I'll never forget last night. I'm glad to be out of this hotel."

The shuttle arrived and was soon heading across town to the apartment they called home. The whole reason for staying at the hotel was to not be disturbed by her brothers and get some alone time. So much for alone time, the night had transformed from wedding night bliss to tears, tragedy, and a hellish menagerie of unfortunate events.

Knowing how Margret hated asking for help from family, Donald winced as he confessed, "I called my Mom and Dad from the hotel lobby. Mom says we can borrow her

Caddy until Wednesday. On Monday, Dad is going to pick up my car for her to drive till we get back."

She looked away from him thinking about how insistent she had been, but at least it was help from his family, not hers. If her brothers had to help she would never hear the end of it. Suddenly she exclaimed, "Oh no. I just thought. All our luggage for the honeymoon is already in the trunk of the car, and the car is locked away. I don't have all the pretty things I got just for the honeymoon."

"No worries. We'll make due. It's not like we don't have other clothes in the closet. We'll find something to wear... or not." He grinned. "Who needs clothes on a honeymoon?"

"Don't be silly. I want to see the caverns at Carlsbad, and I'm pretty sure the entire cave is still a clothing required area." She touched his nose with the tip of her forefinger and said, "The only clothing-optional area will be the motel room at Carlsbad."

He shivered and said, "God, I hope there aren't any cockroaches at this one."

"It's a Howard Johnson Motel. It's supposed to be the best in Carlsbad."

With skepticism oozing from his face he said, "You'd think so, right?"

The shuttle reached its destination, the *Quadruplex Apartments*. Donald had chosen it because of its studio elegance, despite the part of town it was in. Their apartment was one big space with a decorative suspended staircase leading up to an open loft-style bedroom overlooking the single room living area. The housing unit was one of four identical apartments built together so that each of the front doors faced a different cardinal direction. Unfortunately, Donald and Margret's apartment faced the north, providing them with a stunning view of their neighbor's run-down fence.

They unloaded the few bags they had with them, tipped the driver, and arm in arm they walked to the door of the apartment. For the money, Donald considered it exceptionally nice, even if their new neighbors were members of the notorious *Outlaws* motorcycle gang. If nothing else, it was a place they could call home. Margret suddenly froze. There on the doorstep was a pile of rice.

She shook her head and said, "Tommy and the boys got in and did something to our apartment."

With a calm pat on her wrist, Donald replied, "The house was locked. They couldn't get in and breaking in isn't their style. Trust me." He pointed to the lock. "Look. Still locked and no sign of forced entry. Everything's fine. This little pile of rice is just their way of saying, 'Hello. Welcome to your new home.' "

"Okay, if you say so."

He unlocked the door and cussed. The house was a shambles with crepe paper, silly string, and toilet paper draping over everything. The carpet and every fixture had rice in it. They stood in shock.

He said, "How did they get in? I don't understand."

That was when the landlord, Mr. Sykes, popped his head in. He said, "Mrs. Margret, your brother came by yesterday bout 5:30 or so and asked to be let in to get something he forgot. I didn't see how it would hurt and all so I gave him a ke—" He stopped in mid-sentence, gasped, and took in the chaos. "Oh, hell no." Then he saw the suitcases sitting on the step. "You have your clothes packed, you leavin'? Gonna find another apartment after throwin' some wild shindig, leavin' this for old Sikes to clean up? I ain't cleanin' this up. What kind of bachelor party did you have here? This is a wreck. I want it back to its beautiful self today, you hear? That's pitiful... Pi-ti-ful! I ain't havin' this. I'll be back later today to check on it. If it's not spick-and-span— you're out." He spat the words. "You can go find another place to tear up. Not my place."

Donald said, "This isn't from any party. The boys you let in here did this. You need to take some of the responsibility for letting them in when we left it locked."

Margret insisted, "You can't blame us for this mess."

He ignored Margret and looked at Donald when he said, "Hell no. It was her brother and he had a good reason to get in. Said he left his coat in the house, and his flight was leavin' late last night. He needed to just get his coat."

Donald pointed out that it was July, and why would he need a coat in triple-digit temperatures. The landlord waved his hands, turned, and started for the door.

He stopped when Margret said, "So, you gave him the key and he returned it promptly. What you didn't know was he left it open so my brothers and Donald's friends could get back in later to do this."

"Damn, what kind of friends do you have? Mine just send gifts and flowers to weddings." He took another look around and said, "Hell no, this is too much. I'll be back later to see that this is cleaned up, proper like."

It took most of the day to put the apartment right again. They had to clean the petroleum jelly from under every drawer knob, remove the clear plastic wrap from over the toilets. They even found grape jelly in Donald's socks. Then there was the obvious mess left to clean up. There were a dozen trash bags of different kinds of crepe papers, and all their toilet paper had been used to help drape the room. Rice was in every nook and cranny. They vacuumed twice and still found rice here and there.

CHAPTER ELEVEN

The Big Cow Steak House
July 7th, 1979
Saturday
8:00 PM
Lubbock, Texas

Donald and Margret had the apartment looking pretty good when Old man Sykes came by to give his approval. The grumpy landlord was leaving when Donald's parents brought the Cadillac by. It was his mother's pride and joy, a blue Coupe Deville with a white vinyl top. Mom and Dad Wiseman, otherwise known as Martha and Frank, had arrived at the lovebird's love-nest.

Martha commanded, "You take care of my Caddy. You're not going to let Uncle Terry drive it, are you?"

"No mother, it'll just be me and Margret."

She took him aside, only steps away, to the apartment's living room, and in a hushed voice said, "I don't want anyone driving it but you. You hear me. Only you."

"Okay, Mother... only me." Truthfully, he was thinking, *like hell you say. I can't tell my wife to not drive the car because my mother doesn't trust her.*

"Mother, it'll be all right. I promise."

"It had better be. I want it back in the same condition I'm giving it to you."

Martha looked at the multiple bags of trash stacked up waiting to be taken to the garbage. Addressing her new daughter-in-law she said, "Those heathen friends of his got in and tore the place up. Am I right?" She put her arm around Margret. "Your brothers were his friends long before you two started dating. I mean no offense to you, but Dear, they are heathens all the same."

Margret looked down and timidly spoke to her shoes as she said, "Yes, I know, and you're right. They did get in. We've cleaned it up now."

Eager to be a good wife and a good daughter-in-law Margret said, "Can I fix ya'll some supper?" She opened the cupboard. "We have lots of—" She stood there speechless. All the labels had been removed from every canned food in the cupboard. There was no way of knowing what was in any of the cans.

She took two cans out from the bin and opened them with her new electric can opener. "It looks like we're having corn and more corn." She took another random can from the cabinet and opened it. "Dang it, more corn."

Martha had no intention of eating an all yellow meal. "No, no. Forget cooking tonight. You can have mystery food later when it's just the two of you. Dad and I are taking you both out to eat. How about a nice chicken fried steak. The Big Cow is open late and we can just make it if we hurry."

Both Donald and Margret were hungry. They had worked straight through, missing lunch, to get the place back in shape before Mr. Sikes returned for his inspection. As timely and convenient as the invitation was Donald knew they had received it out of his mother's self-interest, not her generosity. Martha's invitation had been motivated by her own hunger and desire to go out to eat. She had no intention of eating a hodge-podge meal, no matter how important it was to Margret. Still, the invitation was too good to pass up, even if it meant Donald would spend more time with his mother.

As they headed for the door, Frank Wiseman asked, "Son, are you two headed to Carlsbad for your honeymoon? I was just asking because of the late start you're getting. There are closer places to have a getaway if you know what I mean?" Then he stuffed a hundred dollar bill into his son's shirt pocket.

Donald replied, "Thanks, Dad. Yes, Margret has her heart set on Carlsbad and seeing the caverns. We'll be back here too quickly, and then it's back to work. You guys have been great. Without help from you and mom, the honeymoon would be a wreck. We'll be off to Carlsbad tomorrow, but right now I'm looking forward to a tasty T-bone from mom's favorite steakhouse."

Mom and Pop Wiseman took Donald and Margret to the Big Cow restaurant and the steaks were as good as promised. It was the first time they had told anyone what bad luck they had at the wedding and especially at the hotel.

Donald said, "You should have seen the bugs. They almost covered the carpet."

Margret chimed in. "They were horrible!"

Frank said, "No thanks. I can tell you one thing your mom would have already filed for divorce by then."

Martha scolded, "Frank, that's not true! I would not. I would've waited till Monday and then called the lawyer."

Margret said, "There'll be no lawyers in our foreseeable future, I assure you." She kissed Donald— more of a peck than a kiss. After all his parents were watching.

"Now, now... that stuff can wait a bit longer," said Frank as he wolfed down the last of his T-bone. Steak sauce dripped onto the top stitching of his modern polyester leisure suit. Trying to clean it off, he wiped at it with his napkin. He showed Martha the stain. "Will this washout?"

Turning sideways in her chair, one foot partially in the walkway between the tables, and leaning over to better inspect his lapel, she scowled. "Frank, the dry cleaners can get it out." She took a closer look and added, "I think."

With a crash, a waiter tripped on Martha's foot and did an uncoordinated and totally ridiculous pirouette which landed him in the middle of the floor; his tray of drinks bathed Donald's lap in iced tea, Dr Pepper, and coffee. Donald couldn't move, mostly from the shockingly cold liquid soaking through to his underwear.

The waiter regained his composure and apologized for the incident saying, "I don't know what happened," and "I'll get the manager."

Martha threatened, "Donald, what did you do this time? Don't you dare embarrass me in here. This is my favorite restaurant. Leave it up to you to make a scene."

"Now Martha, It was an accident. I'm sure the boy didn't do it on purpose."

Donald didn't say anything. He knew from experience that his mother would blame him for it and it was useless to explain. If he wanted to get along with her, he had to keep his mouth shut and take the blame. Especially since he needed to borrow her car to leave on the honeymoon.

Donald excused himself from the table and went to wash the stains out of his shirt and pants. At least as much as he could in a public restroom. The restaurant manager apologized and offered his sincere regret for the accident. His long and agonizing supplication ended with him offering Martha a coupon for two steak dinners of her choice. She took it and told the manager not to worry, it was an accident, and that Donald didn't mean to do it. It was all his fault. When Donald returned from the restroom he was wetter than before.

Donald said, "Margret I think it's time to go."

She agreed and hurriedly collected her purse before she stood.

Frank seemed oblivious to the awkward and uncomfortable position the accident had put his son in. He stood up by the table and continued his conversation as if nothing had happened.

Frank stated, "Donald, I need to talk to you for a minute." He paused as if there was something more to what he had to say before he asked, "What's on the schedule for tomorrow?"

Donald sighed and emotionally surrendered. It was no use hurrying off, he might as well answer. If he just left, he was sure his mother would accuse him of being rude. So, he stayed. "Well, Dad, I've got to have the tux back to the rental shop by 10:30, go by the wedding planner's to pay off the remaining balance for the reception room and the party supplies. Then it's just pick up Margret and head out of town. Carlsbad, here we come."

"I tell you what. You let me take your tux back. You two just sleep in, and start your trip at your leisure."

Margret was the one who spoke up first. "Dad Wiseman, you'd do that? You're the best."

Donald's thoughts were hopeful. *At last, something good. Maybe my luck is changing?* "Thanks, Dad, That'd be a great help. We have reservations at the Howard Johnson in Carlsbad for tomorrow night."

"Good for you, son. Good for you. Don't ever let this one get away. She's a keeper."

"Glad you approve. I sure do."

Martha said, "Frank, if it was left up to you, I have no doubt you'd hum-haw all night and never get it said. Now, you two are making a spectacle of yourselves. Sit down before people start to stare. Donald, your father needs to have a heart-to-heart talk with you before you leave." Margret and Donald obeyed. Why the heck not, he was already soaked to the skin what did it matter if he waited a while longer to dry off. He certainly didn't need his mother upset with him right now.

Donald looked skeptical. "What kind of heart-to-heart talk?"

"Martha, it's not his fault."

"Well, it sure isn't Bob's fault. The man is good as gold."

Donald blurted, "Okay, will someone tell me what's going on?"

Frank said, "We waited to tell you because we didn't want to put a damper on your evening... But, your uncle Bob had a heart attack this morning about 1:00 AM."

Margret was shocked into silence. It was Donald who found the words. "He had just dropped us off at the hotel. What happened?"

Frank opened his mouth to explain but Martha interrupted, and said, "After he dropped you two off he came back to the reception. He and your uncle Terry called Tommy and Marcus out. Said they were going to whip their asses for something they did. It got heated. No blows were thrown though. Probably because right in the middle of the yelling match Bob collapsed. Yep, he grabbed his chest and slumped right over. Had to call the EMS. They took him to Saint Mary of the Plains Hospital. He's okay now. They're just going to keep him a couple days to be sure he doesn't have another one, a worse one."

"How horrible. I'm so sorry," declared Margret.

Martha fussed saying, "Bob is in the hospital because of Tommy and Marcus." Then she turned to Margret and insincerely said, "Honey, their villainy has nothing to do with you personally."

Donald's mother went on to lecture like she had done hundreds of times before, and Margret couldn't blame her for how she felt. It wasn't the first time she had found herself in the crosshairs of her brother's antics, and yet, the point was lost on Donald.

The Michaels brothers were his friends, not Martha Wiseman's; it was just more complicated since he had married into the Michaels family. He would have to deal with whatever fallout came with his choices. As the lecture subsided, and the conversation waned, the newlyweds said goodnight. Donald, mostly dry after his bath of assorted beverages, drove the Coupe Deville to their apartment.

The biker gang who rented the apartment next to theirs were out in the parking lot with tools strewn here and there as they overhauled their bikes. They had taken the apartment door off the hinges, laid it down, and were using it as a ramp so they could get their motorcycles over the porch step and into the apartment.

The newlyweds ignored the gangsters who looked up at them oddly laughing and gleefully watching them walk to their side of the *Quadruplex Apartments* building. This time, when they opened the door, they had yet another surprise. Five bullet holes riddled the wall between their apartment and the one occupied by *The Outlaws*. It was time to call the police.

* * *

Margret and Donald waited for an hour and fifteen minutes for the policemen to arrive. When they came on the scene it was one car with two officers in it.

Donald complained, "Look at this. What if we had been home? They could have killed us."

The older officer, said, "I see. Looks like a forty-five caliber." Then he walked to the far wall and inspected it. "Yep. There are four slugs in the wall on this side."

Officer number two, the younger one, nodded his agreement.

Donald asked, "Well, what are you going to do about it." He had even started waving his hands to emphasize the situation. "Those gangsters live on the other side of this wall. It's obvious they shot through it."

The young officer said, "Yep, looks like that's what they did alright."

The older officer got to the point saying, "I suggest we do nothing."

Donald was horrified and Margret sat wide eyes at his statement. He said, "Nothing—you're going to do nothing?"

The officer insisted, "We can go next door and talk to them, but we have no idea who pulled the trigger. You didn't see who did it, and we'll never be able to make an arrest because these guys won't give up the one who did. If we go over there it'll only make them mad, and you have to live here. They could make your life more difficult than they already have."

Donald said, "That's where you're wrong. I don't have to live here."

The younger officer spoke up and said, "We'd like to help, but honestly there's nothing we can do."

Donald huffed. "I don't know what I was expecting. I guess I thought you would haul them all off to jail." He closed his eyes and silently counted backward from twenty. Counting sometimes helped his nerves. It was something his phycologist had recommended years ago.

Margret said, "Can't you do ballistics on the bullets, and match it with one of their guns?"

The older officer said, "We already know the gun belongs to one of them but they won't say which one. It's pretty hopeless. Ballistics won't tell us anything we don't already know."

Donald said, "If that's everything you can do for us, thanks for nothing. You can go on your way."

Turning to Margret Donald said, "Honey, get all your clothes, and put them in those big black trash bags. We're loading everything up in the car and going to the Best Western for the night. We'll settle this with the landlord tomorrow."

The officers didn't try to convince them they could do anything other than what they had already recommended, however, they did wait in the police cruiser and watch as the newlyweds loaded their belongings into the Coupe Deville.

The gangsters heckled as the newlyweds took load after load of things to Martha's car.

A large biker wearing a bandana for a headband yelled, "What you call big daddy pig for?"

Another one wearing an Outlaws vest yelled, "Thought he might oink you some help?"

The one wearing the headband yelled out, "You thought he would protect you from the bad old bikers?" Then he turned to the waiting cruiser and shook his middle finger at them.

The shirtless one, wearing filthy jeans and straddling his motorcycle, yelled, "Pig lovers, that's what you are... oink, oink." Then he started a chant, "Screw a pig... screw a pig." The others joined in yelling, "Screw a pig... Screw a pig." After a few rounds of even more vulgar jeers he laughed so hard he almost fell off his motorcycle.

The bandana wearing outlaw said, "I hear someone put new air-conditioning in your apartment."

Donald shot him a hard look. "What? You don't appreciate the remodeling. The next tenant will. He'll be one of our brothers. We're taking over this part of town. Hear me? Taking over!"

Donald and Margret didn't say anything. They noticed however that the police kept their distance while the loading took place. With all their clothes packed into several black trash bags and brown paper grocery bags, the honeymooners stuffed the Cadillac full. Margret left barely enough space for her to sit beside Donald on the plush bench seat. It was time to leave the *Quadraplex Apartments* behind, permanently. The police cruiser followed them as Donald drove straight to the *Best Western Motel.*

He looked in his rearview mirror and the cop had turned on his light bar. He pulled over and lowered his driver's side window. The younger of the two officers walked to his door. He had his ticket book out.

The officer said, "Sir, did you know your back left taillight is not functioning." Donald sat in disbelief as the officer proceeded to write out a ticket and have him sign it.

Moments later they pulled up to the Best Western. He used the hundred dollars his father gave him to rent a room for the night.

The motel manager said, "That will be thirty-five out of a hundred. I owe you some change." He opened the cash drawer and remarked, "Of all the luck, my wife just took a deposit to the bank, and I don't have any big bills. I hope you like ones. It seems that's all I have right now." He proceeded to count out sixty-five dollars in one-dollar bills as change for the hundred.

CHAPTER TWELVE

Playing Au Natural
July 8th, 1979
Sunday
9:30 AM
Carlsbad, NM

The Cactus Inn was one of those places that catered to people who wanted to rent a room by the hour. Attached to its long row of seedy rooms, the hotel had a restaurant, bar combination, and since New Mexico wasn't a Blue Law state the bar was open. Even though it was way before noon the hotel restaurant was littered with women who laughed with their eyes and smiled with their legs. Harvard hardly noticed. He didn't have time for entertainment. He sat alone at a table going over the profiles of his new cohorts he compiled and made strategic plans for his upcoming job.

He whispered to himself, "No plan of operation extends with any certainty beyond the first contact against a hostile force." *I've got to be more than thorough, I've got to be totally in these guy's heads.* His thoughts were focused.

Whispering again he said, "I've got to make any apparent escape route a trap." He looked at his satchel like briefcase which held five pounds of plastic explosives. *That should be enough.*

Everything had to be perfect for the events which lay ahead—the dangerous events which lay ahead. He had his mind on business when an abrupt silence demanded his attention.

The chattering women had gone quiet. He looked up to see Katherine Souza standing at his table. In tight black leather pants and a leather halter, she stood out like a magisterial dominatrix in a stable of feeble fillies. She put one of her spiked heels on the pleather seat of the chair beside Harvard and said, "Harvey, you runnin' away from the circus? You don't belong in a whore house. As I recall, you ain't that kind of guy."

He stuffed the papers in his satchel and leaned back in his chair. "As I live and breathe, if it isn't Kat Souza, the Outlaw Bitch of the Texas Outlaws. What brings you out of your litter box and all the way to Carlsbad?" Her appearance meant only one thing, Ruffio was onto him.

Sitting up, he reached out and ran a fingertip lightly over the top of her patented leather pump, up the crisscross laces going down the side of her pant leg, and then brought his fingers to his lips; he licked his fingertips like a kid tasting stolen frosting.

Harvard never failed to entertain, and she was in the mood for some entertainment. Sadly, she had to keep her mind on business—at least for now. "Big bro thinks you have something going on the side." She leaned down seductively. "Do you, Harvey babe? Are you going solo?"

"Kat, you know, doing it solo is never as much fun as when you have a partner." He winked at her. "Are you here because Ruffio sent you to find me, or are you here because you want in on my action?"

She bit her lip in excitement. "So, you do have something you're working on." She batted her eyes and pouted. "It wouldn't have anything to do with those papers you crammed into that oversized scrotum you call a briefcase would it?"

"It might, but you didn't answer my question." He leveled a stare at Kat. "Why are you here?"

"*Mi noivo*, can't a girl catch up with an old flame without getting the third degree?"

"Sweetheart, you haven't been a girl since you were nine years old. I'm looking at Ruffio Souza's number one enforcer, but I have a feeling you're not his puppet."

Kat stepped off the chair and pulled it under her. She straddled it leaning up onto the back with her arms crossed. "*Mi amante,* are you offering a piece of the action? If so, I'm listening."

Harvard knew there was one common dominator among all *The Outlaws*, and that was greed. It was something he could depend on. "I have a lot to offer, but right now, I think we need to retire this conversation to my room. Pillow talk is so much better than shop talk."

"Oh, you do know how to sweet talk a girl. I brought my riding crop, and I'm wearing my stilettos. What else do we need?" She glanced over at the briefcase. "You bring those papers with you and we'll discuss them over a little dessert."

Suddenly Harvard changed his mind. "I have a better idea. Let's have a little dessert in the desert. There's nothing like doing it in the wide-open spaces. I have some blankets in my saddlebags." He stood up in front of her and said, "Leave your Harley here and jump on mine. We can go out in the desert and play *au natural*."

"Harvey, you are a little minx." She stood up, kicked the chair out of her way and walked behind the restaurant's bar. Grabbing a bottle off the top shelf, she looked at it and said, "Johnny Walker Platinum, that'll do. Can't party without refreshments." She strutted as they walked to the parking lot, and asked, "Your hog or mine?"

"Mine. I've got the blankets, remember. Who wants sand in all those hard to reach places?"

"Speak for yourself, Harvey Babe. I can reach all my places just fine." With that, she swung her leg over the back of Harvard's Electra Glide and settled back onto the padded trunk. "You know they call your bike *el coño sobre ruedas*. The rolling pussy." As if she were riding a horse, she slapped the back tire with her crop and laughed.

Harvard replied, "*Un gatito en un coño sobre ruedas*, Kat this is going to be one for the history books."

It was only a few minutes until they were miles out in the desert. Harvard turned down a dirt road to get out of view of the highway. Ahead was a grove of mesquite trees. He pulled the bike over, spread out the blankets next to a young tree, and stripped off his shirt.

Kat had to lay her crop down to strip off her leather halter top. She looked over at him and nodded her approval. He was handsome, bare-chested and reddish-bronze. He slowly rubbed his hands up and down over his jeans. She hurried to undress.

She said, "Harvey, Don't get started without me. Give me a hand with the laces. A girl can't even get out of her own pants without help these days."

He dropped to his knees and said, "All in good time. Kneel with me and let me kiss your shoulders. Let's take it slow." He held a pair of silver handcuffs, running them up and down his bare arms. Metal against his flesh. Pressing hard, he closed his eyes and made sensual moans. "I've been a bad boy. I need punishing."

She dropped down to her knees beside him. "I like the sound of that."

Then he grabbed her wrists and fell on top of her, face to face, nibbling at her neck. She playfully laughed before she realized his deception. In a swift deft motion, he had managed to cuff one of her wrists to the trunk of the three-inch diameter mesquite tree. Its multiple limbs and thorns kept her from pulling the cuffs over the top.

He jumped beyond her reach as she punched at him with her free hand. Yelling, "You *Pendejo*! You motherfu—"

"Now Kat." Interrupted Harvard. "Words never hurt anybody and your claws are not long enough to reach me."

She grabbed her boot knife and started cutting at the tree.

"I'll kill you. I don't care what Ruffio said. I'll kill you."

"Oh my, did he put the kitty on a short leash."

She spat and threw her knife at him. Harvard held her leather halter in front of his face. The blade sliced through but the hilt of the switchblade stuck, hanging up in the leather. Behind the halter, Harvard sighed with relief as the tip of the knife stopped only inches from his nose.

He couldn't resist heckling her. "No... That was me. I put the kitty on a three-inch leash."

Her initial rage had turned to disgust. "That's not the only thing around here only three inches long."

"Kat, don't be rude. Lying never suited you."

"Hear me, Harvard. Run. Run as far as you can, because when I get loose I'm coming for you. I'll kill you. I promise!"

"Run?" He laughed. "I might as well run. You seem to be all tied up at the moment, and I've got a meeting at noon, I can't be late for. We'll dance later." He tossed the bottle of whiskey to her. "Better stay hydrated out here in this heat. You'll dig the metal cuffs through that tree trunk before long."

She screamed, "Harvard, I could die out here before then."

"You're a tough mama. You're the Outlaw Bitch of the Texas Outlaws, remember." He snickered. "Maybe a farmer will find you tomorrow morning when he comes out to plow." He rolled her halter, riding crop, and switchblade together and stuffed them into his left saddlebag. "You know it might be longer than tomorrow morning if those *chi chis* give the farmer a heart attack. You know you have always had quite an impact on men."

"You want an impact. Wait around and I'll give you an impact you'll never forget." She spat again. "You fucker. At least give me back my halter."

"Nope. I need a souvenir to remind me of this day. I have to admit I must be getting slow. I didn't expect to see you here. You completely blindsided me."

"I'll blindside you when I get loose. I'll scratch your eyes out and feed them to you. Then I'll cut off yo—"

"Now, *mi novia*, is that any way to talk to an old flame?" He straddled his motorcycle and yelled back at her as he rode away. "You'd just be in the way, Kitty Kat. There's no place for you on this job."

Shaking her one free fist at him as he left her in a cloud of dust, she yelled back. "Harvey Parker, you're a dead man. You hear me. You're a dead man."

As he rode away she continued to bellow profanity even sailors never heard. He looked back in his rearview mirror. A single finger popped up from her fist.

Harvard rode across town and straight on toward Hobbs. It was only a little over sixty miles and his Electra Glide could make it in about forty minutes. The salesman at Carlsbad's *Friendly Sam's Used Cars* had told him about his brother, friendly Joe, who had just what he was looking for on his car lot. The only thing was *Friendly Joe's Used Cars* was in Hobbs.

In exactly forty minutes Harvard rolled onto *Friendly Joe's Used Car lot*, and although it broke his heart, he did the unthinkable. He traded his new Harley Davidson Electra Glide for a white 1973 Chevy panel truck. It was plain and simple, like a delivery truck. Friendly Joe, in his fast-talking manner, thought he had convinced Harvard of the deal. As always it was all in Harvard's plan.

Friendly Joe said, "You're getting' a real good vehicle in the bargain. This truck is in prime condition. It was used to make deliveries for Jax Bakery here in Hobbs until old Jax traded it in on a car for the misses. Since then it's been settin' on my lot. Used it myself for one thing or another, for a while. Not much call for solid wall panel trucks."

Harvard glared at him in boredom, "Is that so."

"Thought the phone company might want it or something, but no. Seems it was just waiting here for you. You're lucky I had exactly what you were looking for."

"I don't know if I'd call it luck." Harvard looked back at his beautiful Electra Glide and sighed in regret.

Joe had bartered an even swap, motorcycle for the truck. It was what Harvard planned on doing all along, and although he wasn't out any capital, it didn't make him happy. His brand new Harley Davidson motorcycle was worth far more than Friendly Joe gave him by swapping vehicles.

Joe said, "Glad you stopped by, and found the truck you were lookin' for... and right off the bat too. What was it you called it? Oh yeah, when you first saw it, you said it was perfect. I agree it's in perfect condition."

"Whatever you say, Joe." He put his personal feelings aside as he climbed into the driver's seat and started it up. Just like friendly Joe promised the old Chevy sounded like it was in excellent condition.

He stuffed the pink slip into his shirt pocket, and without thanking him for the trade, drove the truck off the lot. If everything went his way, he would be back in Carlsbad by noon.

CHAPTER THIRTEEN

The Indian Casino
July 8th, 1979
Sunday
12:00 Noon
Carlsbad, New Mexico

Carlsbad's Howard Johnson was located next to one of those small Indian gaming rooms scattered across the state. The accessibility to the small casino allowed the hotel to advertise as *A Las Vegas Oasis in New Mexico*. Truly it wasn't like visiting a classy Las Vegas mega-casino, but it was the best thing New Mexico could offer.

The so-called *Howard Johnson Casino* only housed a couple of pool tables, a bingo parlor, a tiny poker room, a tiny smoking room, and some fifteen slot machines. It more closely resembled a fancy pool hall than a casino. To be accurate, the sign said it was an *Apache Gaming Room operated by The Joint Council of Native American Tribes*. The motel chain had taken advantage of the game room's location and built its flagship hotel next to it. Unlike most of the Howard Johnson motels, this new state of the art hotel stood four stories tall and offered amenities the motels weren't capable of. It not only housed the largest of its famous restaurants which the chain was famous for, it provided a bit of grandeur and elegance as it set on the dry sands of New Mexico's desert. As promised in the advertising, one end of the hotel's lobby opened to a covered walkway leading to the gaming room. The guests could walk down a covered concrete path to the separated building. Locals knew the gamming room wasn't affiliated with the hotel, although, the guests might have thought differently.

Inside the gaming room, the distinct sound of gambling filled the smoky air. It was a subliminal recording mixed with the top forty disco tunes being played over hidden speakers. Buzzing and beeping from video slots gave way to the clank of falling chips, and enthusiastic cheers from unseen observers. All this could be heard behind the dance rhythms of ABBA singing about passion and some guy named Fernando.

Four men, playing the penny slots, sat in the back room of the casino called the smoking room. In this room, touristy gamblers could buy tobacco, cigarettes, and cigars from a variety of vending machines and play the cheap slots. Harvard had successfully cleared the room by glaring at the gamblers until they became fearful and went into another part of the casino. Harvard had even closed the glass doors of the smoking room for more privacy. There they sat sipping their BYOB bourbon like the Vegas rat pack. They were gambling, making plans, and talking about how they assumed they were coming into a lot of money.

Harvard put a coin in the *Aces Wild* slot machine and pressed the big red button. The automated bandit began blaring electronic music as the cards on the video screen started whirling. One ace rolled up, another ace, three aces in a row. The bell went off, and the electronic gambling machine ejected a voucher for fifty dollars. It was the most difficult combination listed on the machine's marque.

Without thinking twice Harvard took the coupon, stuffed it in his shirt pocket, changed machines, and continued dropping in coins. Four coins later that machine also rolled out a jackpot. Again, he didn't seem surprised as he stuffed yet another voucher in his pocket. He was bored with it, and his men were arguing. Lighting his Perfecto, he leaned back and listened.

"Harvard has everything worked out. It can't fail," Mika said as he pointed with his glass toward their new leader. The gesture resembled a premature toast because their success had not yet been achieved.

Tarby Thompson leaned against the soft vinyl padding of the chair positioned in front of the slot machine. He replied, "Yep, Harvard says he's been plannin' this for months and nothin's gonna stop us now."

Half listening, Hinto had been sitting at a slot machine feeding it a constant line of coins. He stopped gambling and turned to look at Tarby. He had a decision to make, and it could affect the rest of his life. "I don't know man, the FBI has a way of messing everything up. Maybe we need to go over the details of the job again."

"Harvard couldn't have made it plainer," Tarby replied. "Weren't you listening?"

Mika leaned over to Hinto and said, "Bro, you're not thinking of weaseling out on us, are you? I want my million, and you're not gonna screw it up for me at the last minute."

Tarby said, "This plan isn't for the weak-hearted, Hinto. You and Mika have been working at the cafeteria for over a year now. Way before we met Harvard, they'll never see it coming."

Harvard was puffing on his Perfecto cigar and blowing smoke at his men. They didn't understand it had to go off exactly as he planned it. The risk was astronomical, and he had to convince them—the reward was too. He was, however, keeping part of his plan to himself. They weren't ready for the real reason, for the caper, for what Harvard was sure would be world-shattering news.

They had to think that random fortune had brought them together and any Joe off the street could take their place—taking their million for themselves. It boiled down to a question of who was in charge. If they realized how important they were to his plan, then Harvard would rapidly lose control, and from the first gun fired, to handing out the loot, he must be in control. Everything was planned right down to the last detail, every anticipated response, and every reply. If they could just keep it together for another sixty hours, his men would be millionaires and his message would make him a national hero.

"Hinto, I think you're going deaf. Didn't you hear Tarby when he said, Harvard has it all planned to the last letter." Mika realized he was getting too loud and quieted his yelling to a forceful whisper.

A large Indian wearing a suit and tie started to open the glass doors. Harvard got up and held them shut staring at the man through the glass. The big Indian let go and stood on the outside of the room, staring through the doors. Harvard blew smoke at him from his side of the glass. "What are you gawking at, dip-shit." The words were mouthed more than yelled.

At length, the man let them be and walked away.

"There's nothing that can go wrong. Before midnight Wednesday, we'll each be one million dollars richer." Mika assured Hinto.

Tarby smiled a crooked grin and asked, "Why wait? I want my money now. Mika and I have a couple of shotguns, Hinto has a .22mm rifle, and I've seen Harvard carry his pistol in his belt. We have enough firepower to pull this off tomorrow."

That was enough. This argumentative banter was getting out of control. Harvard held up his hand, stopping the chatter. "No. Boys, we wait till we can do it right. If we go in half-cocked with a menagerie of mishmash weapons we'll look like a bunch of simpletons, just hicks with granny's guns... and everything depends on them taking us serious." He took a sip of his bourbon. "One way to be taken seriously is to use serious weapons. Nobody's going to be laughing at us when we pull this off. Wait till you see them, the guns, I mean. They're real sweet. No news reporter in the world will call us fucking stooges with one of those in hand."

Mika said, "I'm already making a list of all the shit I'm spending my money on."

"What about our exit strategy?" Tarby asked. "There's not many roads leaving Carlsbad, and only two major highways running straight through. If we leave by car, they'll have a motherfucking roadblock out before we get to Las Cruces. If we get caught, nobody will be spending their million."

"Have faith boys. Everything's planned. I promise we'll be flying out of Carlsbad. All you have to do is follow my lead, and I guarantee you'll be spending your million while you sip on one of those little umbrella drinks on a beach in some nonextradition country like Brazil."

Hinto looked over at Mika and asked, "Bro are you sure about this? You think it'll work?"

Harvard was fed up with the vacillation. "If you *vatos* aren't up to the job, I'll find someone else. Maybe one of these *gringos* in this casino has the balls to get a million bucks? I can always ask."

With as much determination as he could muster, Hinto said, "Boss, I can do it. I want my million, and I ain't backing out now."

The men looked at each other cheerfully approving of Hinto's decision to join them.

"Great," Harvard replied. "You just kept me from putting three slugs in your heart and throwing you out in the desert."

They glanced at each other and back to Hinto. "He's kidding," said Mika.

"Hell no. I just sat here and explained what we're about to do. At this point you shitheads are in if you like it or not. All the fucking whining, trying to decide if you're siding with me, like you were joining the damned army or something, is fucking stupid." He took a drink of the liquor. "You're in or you're out... and there's only one way out, and that's in a casket. It don't matter what dead men think, and they sure as hell don't get a million bucks. I'd rather have my money while I can spend it, so, stick with me and that's exactly what you'll do—get a million bucks."

Harvard's men solemnly nodded to each other and made a toast to their impending success. When the glasses clinked together Harvard added, "Of course, if any of you try to be a big shot and take over—I'll just shoot your ass right there and watch you bleed to death."

CHAPTER FOURTEEN

The Best Western
July 7th, 1979
Saturday Night
11:30 PM
Lubbock, Texas

At the Best Western Motel, it was late when the couple finally settled down to rest. At least they were alone and didn't worry about being shot in the middle of the night. Margret cuddled in Donald's arms as they laid back and relaxed from the madness of the last couple of days. He said, "I can hardly believe we're married. All of our misfortunes seem so surreal. I swear if I didn't have bad luck I'd have no luck at all. Are you sure we're genuinely married? Maybe something screwed up and it's not legal."

She replied, "Oh my, that's right. Are you sure we really got married? Maybe we should do the ceremony all over again to be sure."

"Are you crazy? I'm not going through that ever again." He laughed.

"It was sort of like a trip to the dentist, without the Novocain."

"Yes, I suppose it was." He sighed deeply. "But, it's all behind us now."

"Yes, yes, it is. We'll find a place to live as soon as we get back. As a matter of fact, I'll call your dad tomorrow and get him started looking for us a place."

"What happened to your independent spirit and never calling on either of our families for help?"

"I can only handle so much by myself. If we're going on a honeymoon we can't stay here and look for an apartment. I would honestly like to be able to move into one when we get back."

"I'll ask dad to talk to Mr. Sikes and get us out of our lease. Surely he'll give us our deposit back since the apartment is not inhabitable."

She turned to look at him and asked, "Is that a legal term for when gang members shoot up your living room?"

Donald smiled smugly, and said, "Yes, Mrs. Wiseman. Yes, it is." He sighed. "I hope old man Sikes isn't a hard nose about this. We sure could use at least a part of the deposit to put down on another place. Maybe he'll evict them, and we can stay there." They looked at each other and laughed.

Margret said, "Not a chance. He'll piss his pants just talking to those guys. He can get away with bullying us because he knows we won't pull a gun on him, but he'll be completely a different person when he talks to them. He's probably so scared of them, I bet he doesn't even ask for the rent. No, he's not evicting them. We'll find a better place. Just wait and see."

In the solitude of their motel room, for once, Donald and Margret had a few minutes to themselves. Margret slipped off her negligée and Donald stepped out of his Jockey shorts. Together they snuggled under the covers. Things were getting hot when they were abruptly interrupted by a loud series of knocks. Someone incessantly stood outside pounding on their door.

Donald got up and struggled to put his tighty whiteys back on before answering the door. He kept getting his foot in the wrong leg opening. After some pulling, stomping, and swearing, his bits and pieces were covered enough for him to angrily throw the door open.

"What is it?" Donald howled.

A disheveled man smelling of stale urine answered him. "Hey, Buddy." The drunkard staggered backward and only managed to regain his balance before falling. "I'm looking for my friend Sonny. He invited me to a party, and said it was at this place, in this room."

Donald in a mild yell replied, "There is no party here." Then he slammed the door.

The man banged on the door again as Donald slipped off his underwear and climbed back into bed.

Margret asked, "What was it? What's going on?"

"Nothing dear. It's a drunk who claims he was invited to a party. Thinks it's in this room. Ignore him. Now, where were we? Oh yes."

Thud, thud, thud, the drunk pounded on the door.

"Can't he see the lights are out? The only party here is a party for two."

"We know that, but this guy won't quit."

Wham, wham, wham, the drunk pounded on the door.

"Send him away, please," she begged.

Donald got up and again hurriedly struggled to put the right leg in the right place in his underwear. Awkwardly, he managed to pull them up before he lost his balance. Then he hurried to the door.

The pounding had stopped by the time Donald flung the door open a second time. No one was there. Donald leaned out of the doorway and looked one way and then the other, but there was no sign of the drunk.

Closing the door again he said, "Looks like he left." He hurried over to the bed and started to pull his underwear down.

"That's enough of that for tonight, Dear. I'm so tired. Let's just sleep."

Disappointed, Donald climbed back under the covers, underwear and all. Suddenly, bam, bam, bam, someone was knocking again. He jumped out of bed and threw open the door to find the motel's night manager standing on the other side of his threshold.

The manager scolded, "What do you think you're doing? At this motel, guests don't stand in the doorway in their underwear like a lude pervert. This is a respectable place. I also have a complaint about you banging on the walls."

Donald was stupefied and couldn't say anything.

"Well, what do you have to say for yourself? We don't allow streakers here. If this is a party prank you can pack up and head down the road."

"No, Sir. This is... I mean we aren't having a party. This drunk came by and was banging on the door."

"What drunk? I don't see a drunkard."

"He left, but he was here. Ask my wife. Honestly, he was here banging on the door."

"And, I suppose he made you answer the door in this unsuitable attire. Don't just stand there in your birthday suit. Get some clothes on, for heaven's sake."

Donald stepped back inside to slip on his pants. "I wasn't naked when I answered the door. I was wearing my underwear. It's no different than wearing a swimsuit."

"You don't get to say what the moral code is for guests at my hotel." He was howling louder than Donald had at any time before, but there was no arguing with the man. Donald came back wearing his pants.

"There that's better. We can have a decent conversation now."

"I'm sorry about the banging, and I won't be standing where people can see me when I'm only wearing my underwear—I promise. All we want is to get some sleep."

"Alright, see to it this doesn't happen again. No more complaints, hear me? Just cause it's 1979 doesn't make immoral behavior proper. Streaking and flashing then calling out *hey Ethel see this*, people of real moral fiber don't do those kinds of things." He sighed. "Just calm down and you can stay till morning. Still, if I get any more complaints, then I'll be back with the law. No matter what time of the morning it is, you'll spend the next day in jail."

Margret yelled from inside the room. "We promise, really we do."

"You better. I'll be watching you, young man. Yes, I will. I'll be watching." He turned and went back to the manager's suite.

Donald slipped back under the covers to get some sleep. Granted, it was only four hours of rest, but it was something.

The next morning they reloaded their bagged luggage into the car. Then they got breakfast from the IHOP around the corner, and mailed a greeting card to the pastor, thanking him for his generosity in providing the chapel without cost. Margret indeed called Donald's father asking him to start looking for an apartment for them and to please try to get their deposit back.

It was an uncomfortable call for Margret because upon hearing her rendition of the bullet holes and what the police said, Frank Wiseman yelled and cussed the gang members, as well as, the police too. Time was passing and at 12:30 PM they were still in town. After getting a quick lunch at the *Bonus Burger*, they headed to Carlsbad.

Donald waited in the car for what seemed an eternity, but it was worth the wait. When Margret reappeared she looked like a million bucks in her canary yellow bell-bottom slacks and printed cream-colored Rayon blouse. Dressed like that, she could have been going to *Studio 54* to hear the Bee Gees perform live. She ran her hand over the leather upholstery of the Cadillac. Its luxury was vastly superior to the cracked vinyl seats of Donald's little Ford Pinto.

It was 2:00 PM and they were just inside city limits, driving on the freeway, heading out of town. At last, they were carefree, two young people in love starting their honeymoon and out of the blue, the car died going down the road. They managed to safely weave through traffic, and get to the road's shoulder before it coasted to a stop. In the rearview mirror, Donald noticed a red mustang pulling behind them as they pulled onto the shoulder of the road. At least the interstate had a nice wide shoulder, however, it was a meager consolation because Donald's curse had struck again.

It was time to call Donald's dad for help. If anyone could get it going... he could.

In the rearview mirror, Donald saw a woman wearing too much makeup and chunky beads get out of the mustang. When he got out of the caddy she was standing directly behind it.

She yelled, "You cut me off you stupid, shit-faced, son of a bitch. What gives you the right to cut in front of me in traffic? I had to stomp on my breaks to keep from running over your skinny ass."

Donald started to explain, "Ma`am, I'm so—"

She cut him off in mid-sentence. "You ain't going to talk over me. I'm of a mind to make a citizen's arrest right here. Do you know, a traffic violation in the lovely state of Texas is a mist-o-meanor crime? You might as well have shoplifted something. If I had my bag phone in the car I'd have the police on the telephone now. You... you just lucky." She fumed with anger. "That's what you are. No one fucks with Sally Harmsworth."

"I'm not trying to fuck with you."

"So, now you're getting fresh. Sexual harassment that's what this is." She started yelling at the moving traffic. "Sexual harassment here. This man wants to fuck me. I'm in danger. Help." She waved her arms to get someone to stop. "Help. Rape."

Then Margret started crying.

Sally blurted, "What's that I hear? You have some unsuspecting female in there with you?" She turned to the traffic again and screamed, "Double rape."

Margret stepped out of the car. Tears streaming down her cheeks.

"Come over here to Sally. That brute won't hurt you, not anymore. Missy, tell Sally all about it."

Margret said, "We had no choice but to cut you off in traffic. The car died. Donny was lucky to get it pulled over at all. By all rights, we should have wrecked." She wiped her eyes with her handkerchief. "We're already one day late starting our honeymoon. Everything is happening wrong. There were cockroaches at the hotel... cockroaches I tell you, and on my wedding night," Margret billowed tears as she talked.

"Oh my, you lousy motherfucker. Making your bride stay at a roach motel on her wedding night, what kind of a cheap-ass son of a bitch are you?"

Donald didn't know what to say. First, he was a traffic criminal and then he was a rapist. She was turning everything he said against him.

"You just gonna stand there or are you gonna say something on your own behalf." Then she turned, nodded toward Margret, and said, "Little honey here ain't putting up with any more of your shit. I'm taking her to a women's shelter right now."

"I didn't do anything!"

With her cheeks still wet, Margret said, "It's true. None of this is Donald's fault it has just been the wedding weekend from hell."

"Honey, I understand completely. Marriage transition can be difficult. You can tell Sally what's wrong, He's too big for you, isn't he. That happens, it only means you're sexually incompatible. Divorce him now before things only get worse."

"No." Margret finally yelled. "Please get in your car and leave. We are all right! We'll call a wrecker for the car. Everything is fine."

Sally huffed, "This is the last time Sally tries to do something good for someone. I can tell what kind of man he is. He's no good. I'm telling you right now. You just wait, you'll remember Sally when you have five kids and your boobs hang to your knees. You'll wish you'd taken Sally's advice." With that, she shut the door to her car and drove back into traffic.

With Sally on her way, the only thing on Donald's mind was how he had to get to a telephone. So, they left the car on the roadside. From where they were on the freeway, it was three blocks across a small cotton field over to the Saint Mary of the Plains Hospital. A relatively short hike to a telephone and to ask Donald's dad for help... again.

They traversed the field in their disco duds. The half-grown, well-watered, cotton plants incessantly reached up and snagged Margret's disco slacks, and for Donald, the soft ground was hell to walk on as he was wearing his inch high platform soled loafers that sank in the mud up to the top of the sole with every step. They emerged from the field less pristine than when they entered, but determined. To their surprise, Frank's old Chevy truck sat in the parking lot outside the hospital. Frank and Martha were there visiting Uncle Bob in his hospital room. After Donald knocked the mud off his shoes they went in to find his parents.

Frank saw them coming down the hall toward Bob's room and stepped out in the hallway to caution them not to excite Uncle Bob, but before he could say a word they erupted with emotion as they told of the latest in their ongoing saga of unfortunate events.

Once he was able to get a word in edgewise Frank said, "Donald, Margret – not a word to Aunt Lolly or Uncle Bob about that phone call we had earlier. I don't want to hear anything about gunshots or bullet holes. We'll take care of that later. No sense getting Uncle Bob riled up. Just put it out of your minds for now. I promise I'll get that situation taken care of. You don't worry a bit. As for you two getting out of town, you take my truck and I'll get your mother's old bucket of bolts running again. Now, Bob and Lolly knows you're here. We could see you walking down the hall. So, come on in his room, visit a bit, and then I'll bring the Caddy back to the hospital while you two are safe and sound in my old truck."

They entered Bob's room, He greeted Uncle Bob and Aunt Lolly with a bright smile. Donald gave his mother a grimaced grin before he turned his attention to Bob and said, "They tell me your heart needed a kick start."

"The old things not even as stout as a can of beer these days," replied Bob. "But, don't fret about me. I'm fine. Needed a little rest. That's all."

Margret said, "It's just good to see you sitting up and smiling."

"We can't stay we're trying to leave for our honeymoon," said Donald. "We were in mom's Caddy and it broke down on the highway."

Martha shot him a look Donald thought was filled with fiery daggers and flying lead. She started to say something but Frank cut her off.

"Now Martha, I told the kids they could take the truck and I'd get the Caddy."

She replied, "Well, get to it then, Donald. Take him to get my car at once. I don't want my baby on the street unprotected. Shoo... go!"

She cocked her head to the side, pressed her lips together, and twisted her face into what Donald had always called his mother's insistent face. Truth be told, it made her look more like a prune with lipstick.

No matter what she looked like Donald knew what her expression meant. It was like he could hear her in his head complaining. *Who was driving? I bet that woman you married did something to my car. This is not how I gave it to you, and I told you I wanted it back in the same condition I gave it to you. Donald, you never do anything right. If it's not one thing it's another. You've been a loser all your life, and marriage hasn't changed you one iota.*

As expected, when she did speak she wanted to know who was driving.

Frank said, "Martha, that's not important now. We gotta get these kids out of town today."

She huffed, "Look what you did. I gave you my car and now it's broke down. Who knows what's wrong with it. What if your father can't fix it? What then?"

Frank gave her a stern look and said, "Martha, that's enough. We don't want to get Bob upset."

Aunt Lolly said, "Martha, you stay here with us and let Frank take care of the problem. We don't want to get Bob too stirred-up. It's important to keep him calm."

"You're so right, Lolly. You know I disapproved of them taking it all along." She cut her eyes toward her husband. "I'll stay here and keep Bob calm while Frank gets my Caddy back to me." Her voice was growing in intensity as she spoke through gritted teeth.

She walked out into the hall with them as they were leaving. Her final words were, "Don't think this is over young man. Your father told me about the bullet holes. What did you do to make them so mad at you?" She sighed... relaxed her shoulders and said, "Whatever you did to those poor motorcycle boys, I think you should apologize and make friends with them. Your father has better things to do with his time than to find you an apartment."

Frank calmly replied, "I said, that's enough Martha. We'll discuss it later."

Donald and Margret didn't wait around for more bickering. They left.

It only took a few minutes to get Frank Wiseman to the Cadillac. He said, "Don't take anything your mother says to heart. This thing is on its last leg. I simply don't want to make payments on a new one. You know she thinks she must have a Caddy because our neighbor has one." He jumped into the driver's seat and turned the key. Like magic it started, then died again. After a little peddle pumping, it started and roared to a constant idle.

"Is that all it needed?" Margret asked.

"She's a contrary bucket of bolts, this one." He paused. "Gotta treat her just so, and she'll set up and do tricks for ya."

"Ha... I'd like to see that," said Donald.

"You two go ahead and take my truck. It's definitely more reliable than this overrated Chevy." He scratched his head. "I'm not sure why she died in the first place. She might do it again."

Donald said, "I think one of the fates doesn't want us going on a honeymoon."

Margret replied, "That's just too darned bad. We've only got a couple of days now. So, we better get going." With everything ready, they threw only a couple of trash bags into the back of the truck leaving the backseat of the Coupe Deville loaded, and left on US 62 towards Carlsbad via Brownfield, Seminole, and Hobbs. If the truck could manage the short two hundred mile journey they would arrive later today.

CHAPTER FIFTEEN

Russian Made Rifles
July 9th, 1979
Monday
Noon
Carlsbad, NM

Harvard walked into *Groovy Jay's Pawn Shop*. His mood was sour and demanding. He had traded his precious Electra Glide for a panel delivery truck. The very thought of it made him mournful. There was one advantage, Kat rode right by Harvard as he drove the truck and she didn't realize it was him. She would be searching the whole town for his precious Electra Glide.

Jay, the owner of the pawnshop, bent down to polish the glass on one of his display cases when he heard the bell on the door and yelled, "Can I help you." Then he stood up. "Oh, it's you." He looked around, a nervous twitch pulled at his left eye. "I guess you want that order you put in."

Harvard made a grunting sound then said, "Damn right. Is it ready?"

"Yeah man. It's in the back." He opened the gate, and let the lugubrious customer behind the counter of the pawnshop.

The shop owner grabbed a box of the special order Russian 5.45x39mm shells and showed Harvard the way to the stockroom. There, among a cluttered mess of stacked boxes and tarp-covered crates, was a long wooden box. Jay popped the top open with a crowbar and pulled the straw packing from around four Russian made Kalashnikov AK-74 Assault Rifles.

Jay said, "These are the newest thing in assault rifles. Forget the old AK-47 model these are lighter and more powerful. Right after you made your order my source got busted. You can tell Ruffio Souza, he owes me big for this one."

Harvard smiled letting him think the guns were for *The Outlaws*. What Jay didn't know didn't hurt him. To continue the ruse, Harvard nodded at the right times, silently complimenting jay's connections and his underworld sources.

Jay pompously bragged, "I didn't think I was going to swing the deal for a while, but never let it be said Groovy Jay let *The Outlaws* down. Yep, these babies were hard to get, but they pack a whopping punch in their compact size. Like I said they're smaller than the AK-47s with a barrel length of only sixteen inches. And, weighing in at only seven and a quarter pounds, these little mamas can deliver six-hundred and fifty rounds per minute. Don't let their size fool ya. This AK-74 is a serious weapon meant for serious business."

Harvard took one from the crate, and with a scowl, unsnapped the clip. The ammunition looked different than he expected.

"I can see you know your guns. The bullet you're holding is a Russian made 5.45x39mm shell. As you know the AK-47's use 7.62x39mm which takes up more room than this one. What all this means is you get more bullets in the clip and don't need to change clips as often."

Harvard asked, "Okay. I get it, but is it going to be a problem finding shells?"

"Don't worry, I got nine hundred rounds for you. Running out of ammo in the middle of a heist wouldn't be cool, man. Don't worry about reliability either, these little mammas work just as well as the AK-47s. They never stick or jam. First one rolled off the production line four and a half years ago, so believe me when I say these are the newest, and the best Russian made automatic assault rifles on the market."

Harvard inspected the boxes of ammunition, and with a smile indicating he was pleased with it, loaded the clip, snapped it back on, and pulled the bolt letting the shell slide into the chamber. It worked perfectly. The only thing left would be to fire it to get a feel for the recoil, however, the back of a pawn shop in a well-populated part of town was not the place for target practice. He would drive his men outside of the city to finish testing them.

Jay said, "Why so glum? I thought you'd be glad to get these babies. I had a hard enough time laying my hands on them."

"Glum? Whose glum? I've got a lot on my mind, that's all." Giving Jay his best movie star smile, Harvard looked up, winked and said, "I'll pull the truck around back and load 'em up."

CHAPTER SIXTEEN

The Men from the Potash Mine
July 8th, 1979
Sunday
6:30 PM
On Highway 62

Donald and Margret were making good time as they flew down the highway toward what they believed would be a perfect honeymoon at the Carlsbad Howard Johnson. Only moments ago they crossed the Texas–New Mexico state line where Central Time became Mountain Time and they set their watches back an hour.

Margret said, "Our trip'll feel like it was only four hours when in fact it was five."

Donald replied, "Wishing isn't going to make sundown any later. The only places in Carlsbad open after 7:00 will be a couple of restaurants, some gas stations, that new gaming room, and the Howard Johnson."

Suddenly startled, Margret looked up. "Donny, do you hear something?"

"Hear what?"

"I hear a hissing sound?"

"Don't start with hearing sounds. Last time it brought on a calamity."

"No, seriously... I hear something hissing maybe spewing."

Instantly the truck started coughing and sputtering. The temperature gauge shot over to hot and jets of steam sprayed from underneath the hood. Donald pulled over onto the shoulder of the highway and killed the engine. Exasperated he jumped out of the cab and threw up the hood. Billows of steam gushed out toward his face. Coughing and waving his hands he managed to fan the fog away from around the engine.

Margret was hanging out of the truck's window yelling to him. "Donny, what's wrong with it?"

He leaned over the fender and yelled back to her. "Looks like a hose busted."

She had retrieved her linen handkerchief from her overnight bag, the only piece of real luggage she had with her and was blotting the perspiration off her face. "Can you get it started?"

Donald kicked the tire as if banging the rubber was the magic fix. "Not without ruining the engine."

"Oh. Well, that's not good, is it?"

"No. That's certainly not good."

Margret got out of the truck and walked to where Donald was leaning against the headlight. He was holding his head and saying a prayer. She put her arms around him.

"What are we going to do now?" She tilted her head and asked, "Are you praying for the car to start?"

He slammed the hood down and replied, "Not exactly." He walked back to the driver's seat, pressed the auto-lock and closed the door. "How's your thumb?" he asked.

Margret looked skeptical. "What do you mean?"

"There's only one thing to do and that's hitchhike to Hobbs. It's only about twenty more miles ahead."

"Hitchhike?" She almost swallowed the word as she said it.

"Unless you want to wait here while I catch a ride into Hobbs and make my way back with a new hose."

She looked around at the desolate landscape surrounding Highway 62. "No. I'm not staying here by myself. I'm going with you." She used her headscarf to tie her hair into a ponytail then pulled her white handkerchief under her belt tucking it into the waistband of her yellow bell-bottoms.

On any other day, the highway would have been busy with traffic. This wasn't any other day. They walked west on the gravel shoulder and put their thumbs out for the few cars flying past them. For an hour, no one stopped. Then a convertible whizzed by with three jeering boys in it. They threw a beer bottle at Margret as the car passed. A second later they pulled over to the side of the road waiting for the hitchhiking couple to catch up to where they were.

"Donny, I don't like this. These guys scare me. I don't want to go anywhere with them."

"We don't have to. We can just stay back here, and let them get tired of waiting for us. In a few minutes, they'll just drive off."

Contrary to Donald's prediction, the car didn't drive away. It sat in silence. The jeering boys faced frontward. Not one of them looking back yelling as they had done when they passed.

Nervously Margret said, "They're not leaving. What now?"

"We walk back toward Dad's truck."

Suddenly the passenger side door of the car opened.

She looked at Donald. "I'm tired of walking. Maybe they're not as bad as they seemed. We could ask them to take us to Hobbs."

"I don't like this. I don't think they want to take us anywhere."

"They opened the door. They mean for us to get in."

"Okay, we'll talk to them."

They turned toward the car and walked together, ever so casually, until Donald could touch the back fender. When he did the young men turned around all at once and yelled at them.

"Fuck you, ass hole."

The driver slammed onto the accelerator pedal and peeled away, sprayed them with gravel.

The honeymooners stood there, in a puff of exhaust, and with their arms protecting their faces.

Margret said, "I've decided I don't like hitchhiking."

"I'm not fond of it either, Love. But, what else are we supposed to do?"

"My guess is that we walk to Hobbs. It can't be much farther."

"We might make it there by sundown."

It was getting on into the afternoon when what looked like a utility truck stopped for them. The flatbed had wooden side rails and a canvas canopy covering the entire back. Being a company truck it didn't have air-conditioning and was running with the radio blaring and the windows down.

Margret said, "About time someone stopped who's a decent person."

"Wait here and let me talk to him."

Donald ran to the passenger side window and asked, "Can you give us a ride." To his surprise, there were three ash covered men setting across the bench seat. The only place on their face not covered with soot was around their eyes, where they had been wearing goggles, and a strip of flesh showed across their mouth and noses, where they had worn some cloth or filter. Everywhere else, clothes, hands, hair, neck, and ears were all covered with black soot. Shocked, he backed up a bit and looked at the signage on the side of the truck door. It read: *Alderson's Potash Mining.*

Margret impatiently ran up beside Donald. Before looking into the cab she said, "Thank you so much. You're the first to stop for us. A car full of boys stopped earlier, but they pulled away before we could get in. I guess most people are afraid of picking up stra—" Upon seeing the men, she stopped short and made an audible gasp.

The driver yelled, "There's no room up here, but you and your misses are welcome to jump in the back."

Margret and Donald stood appalled at the sight of the strange men.

He smiled. The contrast of his white teeth against the soot-covered skin was a bit eerie. "I don't think you'll be a problem." The workmen laughed. "Are you getting in or not?"

Conquering his uneasy misgivings about the situation, Donald nodded at Margret and opened the back flap of the truck. Inside were six more soot-covered men sitting on makeshift seating attached to the truck's bed. All were big, brawny, and dirty.

With sooty hands, they helped Margret and Donald into the back and made room on the dirty make-shift bench seats. One of the big men asked, "What happened? Did ya'll break down?"

Margret wanted to be sarcastic. The first reply she thought of was, *No. I love putting my life in danger by getting a ride with nine rank strangers covered with greasy ash and setting on dirty seats, ruining my clothes.* What she actually said was, "Thank you so much for stopping. We've been walking for miles." It was then when the tears started. She couldn't help it. They started and wouldn't stop. She clung to Donald's arm and buried her head into his chest as she cried.

Another of the brawny men said, "Missy, we don't mean to scare ya. We're headed to Hobbs and we'll help you get going again. No kidding, we will."

Donald sighed and said, "This has been a trying weekend. We're just married as of Friday." Once he started talking, the story of the whole horrible dilemma came flowing out. The men sat there listening and shaking their heads. Donald laughed at the fact of them having had one trouble after another and listening to him laugh about their harrowing tale strangely made Margret feel better. She joined Donald in his storytelling mania by telling her version of the tale.

The man who helped them into the back of the truck said, "It's about time you two caught a break. I'm so glad it's us who picked you up."

Another man said, "We're here. Hobbs city limits."

The driver drove each man to his home and when the last workman jumped out of the truck he went to the driver while Donald and Margret waited alone on the sooty bench. The potash-covered man stood at the driver's window for a long while talking to him before he returned to Donald and Margret waited. He caught ahold of the side rail and swung himself up onto the back like a kid playing on the monkey bars at the park. The big man said, "Gerald is the driver and he's going to take you to Gibson's Discount Center. They have some automotive parts like hoses and such. The only auto parts house in town closes at 8:00, and it's 8:00 now. Anyway, Gibson's will probably have what you need. He'll drop you off, but after you get the part, wait there, and we'll be back to pick you up to take you to your truck."

"Thanks... I don't even know your name," said Donald.

"It's Eric, Eric VanNess." He smiled a queer grin, his white teeth showing between curved soot-covered lips. "You better get going." Then he jumped down, slapped the back of the truck, and signaled the driver who headed off toward the store.

A big storefront with an illuminated sign announced they had arrived at the *Gibson Discount Center.* The sign advertised *Every Thing a Body Needs in One Place, Your One Stop Shopping Treat.* The parking lot was almost as big as the store. On one side of the parking lot was an open field with a sign announcing it to be the future site of something called a K-Mart and on the other was a derelict Texaco gas station, the victim of either a bad economy or bad management.

Gerald said, "They should have a simple water hose. I'll go home and change and be back real soon. Wait for me at the front door by the Gibson's sign."

Margret got out of the truck and dusted off as much of the greasy soot as she could from her blouse and yellow slacks. Donald said, "Okay. We'll be watching for the truck."

"No. I'll park the truck when I get home. I'll be back in my Chrysler. I'll honk three times and flash my lights. If you don't hear me I'll wait a bit and honk again."

Margret said, "No worries. We'll be watching." She was still trying to dust off the sticky greasy soot, but only managed to smear it across her perfectly made-up face. Donald didn't look any better. He had streaks of potash across his forehead, under his nose, and on his cheek.

Donny and Margret looked on every shelf in the Gibson Discount Center's automotive department. Donny said the truck was a small block and needed a 1 ¾ inch diameter hose about 12 inches long. Such a small thing and yet it had them stopped dead. He also said they needed antifreeze and water for the radiator. She found the hoses, but they were all 2 ½ inches in diameter.

She said, "Does it have to be 1 ¾ inch? Can't you make this one work?" She held out the wrong size hose to him.

"No. It has to be the 1 ¾ inch or we'll be stopping in a few miles to do it all over again."

"I can make a dart in it like I do when I sew. That'll make it smaller at the opening."

"No, it won't work. It'll spew steam from the crack. Sorry, Babe. It has to be the 1 ¾ inch size hose."

"I don't understand why they don't have one."

"These are radiator hoses for a tractor. I guess they do a lot of farming here and need a ton of tractor hoses."

She was starting to feel the desperate hopelessness of their situation. "What do we do now?"

"Gas stations usually have them too." He tried to sound as cheerful as possible. "Surely a gas station will have the size we need."

Hand-in-hand Donald and Margret waited for Gerald at the front of the store. They were loitering and looking through the plate glass hoping he would show up at any moment, but time passed and he hadn't returned. It was 9:00 and the store was closing. The security guard ushered them out into the parking lot to wait. Still, there was no sign of Gerald. In the distance, the sound of thunder signaled an approaching storm, and soon, raindrops were falling in slow erratic patterns. Margret leaned closer to Donald and started to sob again.

"We'll be alright," Donald softly cooed. "To me, Gerald seemed reliable. I think he'll be here soon."

"But we're getting all wet."

"Look." Donald pointed toward the derelict Texaco gas pumps across the parking lot. "We can at least get out of the rain over there under the canopy."

Together they ran for the gas station as the sprinkling rain turned into a full-fledged summer shower.

They scurried to the shelter, taking moments of time to dance around in the rain like naively innocent children. The gas station was dark and vacant with an *out of business* sign on the door. Two pumps stood in front of the derelict station like unarmed sentinels. The rain instantly turned the heated evening into a cool respite and the temp was still dropping. Under the fourteen-foot tall metal carport, the couple huddled together near the glass door where the rain couldn't touch them.

She whispered to him, "This will be the oddest place I've ever spent the night, crouching outside a deserted gas station."

"Oh no. No, wife of mine is going to spend the night outside a gas station in the rain."

"Oh really? And, what pray tell are you going to do?"

It was then a dark blue Chrysler New Yorker pulled around the building and up to the pump in front of the couple. The dark-tinted window lowered. It was Gerald and Erik. Surprisingly, they were washed and dressed in clean clothes, and all but unrecognizable except for their voices.

Gerald called over to Donald, "You can't stay there. You'll be arrested for vagrancy." He laughed. "Get in."

It didn't take a lot of convincing for Donald to run to the car and open the back door so his bride could slide inside. She said, "Were just filthy. We'll get your seats all messed up."

"Don't worry about that. They'll clean. It wouldn't be the first time potash has been on them."

Donald said, "We'd almost given up on you."

Erik replied, "Yeah, sorry about that. It took longer than I expected, and this rain came out of nowhere. Gerald made some calls to filling stations and even this Gibson Discount Center here. I'm guessing you didn't find one because they said they didn't have any 1 ¾ inch hoses. The store manager said he didn't even have a 2-inch hose." He shook his head and sighed. "I can't imagine no one has it. Everyone in town is overstocked with tractor parts. Talk about bad karma. I mean it's a common item, after all. It looks like we'll have to wait till morning and get it from the auto parts store."

Donald gritted his teeth and mentally blamed his curse. It had struck again.

Margret looked confused, and asked, "Does that mean we spend the night here in your car?"

He laughed, "Hell no. The boys and I got together and pitched in for a wedding present for you two. It was what took us so long. We're putting you both up for the night at the La Quinta Inn on Highway 62. It's not real fancy, but it's clean— no cockroaches, I promise."

Margret started crying again.

Erik exclaimed, "Oh hell!" He leaned his arm across the back of the New Yorker's front seat and spoke with concern. "What's wrong now?"

She said, "Nothing... it's just so sweet." She was blotting her eyes with her overused handkerchief.

Donald said, "You guys would do that?... And, you don't even know us."

Gerald replied, "After tellin' us your story we decided you deserved a break. I hope this renews your faith in people. At least a little bit."

They drove to the little motel located on Highway 62 where they had checked Donald and Margret in for a one night stay. Erik said, "I know it'll be early, but our shift starts at 8:00 AM and it's an hour's drive to the mine. The auto parts store opens at 6:30 AM so, if you'll be ready, we'll pick you guys up at 6:00 for breakfast. Then we'll get the part you need, and take you back out to your truck."

Donald hadn't thought about the safety of his dad's truck. "Do you think it'll be safe out there on the highway?"

"I don't know for sure. I think it'll be all right. You can call a wrecker and have them pick it up and bring it to the motel, but they'll charge out the wazoo because it's so late and then remember this is Sunday. That changes the wrecker's rates. It'll be time and a half for working on Sunday."

Donald made the decision to leave the truck until they could get back with the hose. They said their goodnights and the men left the lovebirds to themselves. This time no broken pipe made them change rooms and no plague of roaches waited to ambush them. It was just as promised, a normal room in a nice clean hotel.

Donald Showered and came out of the room's bathroom wearing his towel. "Ready or not here I come." As he ran over to where she sat on the bed.

Sadly, to Donald's dismay, Margret was emotionally and physically drained. "Honey, I just don't feel it. I know I promised to make this a clothing-optional night, but I didn't foresee all this. Our *au natural* adventure will just have to wait until another night."

"Okay, Dear. It was a long walk after all."

*   *   *

The wakeup call came too early for the newlyweds. They slowly stirred and put themselves together for the day. Without their luggage, they purchased a few items such as toothbrushes and deodorant from the handy vending machines the motel made available for their guests. There was sadly nothing they could do about having to wear the same clothes as the day before. At least they could be waiting for Gerald at 6:00 AM as promised.

Margret said, "Donny, We better hurry up. They'll be here soon. What's taking you so long?"

"Nothing, just thinking. I hope our things are still in the back of the truck."

"I'm sure they will be," Margret said. "Everything's in those garbage bags and they sure don't look like luggage." She took one last look at her once fluffy hair. "Okay. I'm ready."

Donald reached for the hook style door handle. He pressed down. It didn't open.

"What's wrong now?" Margret asked.

"It's stuck. It won't open."

Exasperated, she exclaimed, "Oh, just stand back and let me do it." Margret twisted the handle every way she could. It wouldn't budge.

"Stand aside, dear," Donald said. "I'll hit it, and maybe it'll unstick." He whacked at it with the side of his fist. It wouldn't open. He took off his shoe and hammered at it. Nothing made it open.

Margret was getting beside herself with impatience. "I don't get it. It opened fine last night. This is ridiculous."

Donald replied "I'm just as fed up as you are with all the hiccups, but there's nothing to do about it except call the manager. I feel certain he'll be able to get it open."

Donald called the manager, in only a few minutes he was there with a master passkey.

The manager yelled through the door, "Mr. and Mrs. Wiseman, Are you there? Can you hear me?"

"Yes, we're here." Margret blurted. "How can we go anywhere when we can't get out?"

"Yes, I see your point. I'm so sorry about this. Believe me, nothing like this has ever happened before."

Donald whispered under his breath. "I bet it hasn't. Not till I got here."

Margret asked, "What was that, Dearest? Did you say something?"

Donald said, "I said, I bet he gets us out of here."

"I know that, Dear. Don't worry, we'll be waiting for Eric in no time."

The Manager tried everything he could think of. At length he said, "I hate to ask you to do this, but could you two go to the window and open it."

Donald tried to turn the lock on the window. It wouldn't budge.

In only moments the Manager appeared on the other side of the glass.

"It won't open."

"What?" The Manager pounded on the window frame and said, "Try opening it again."

Still, Donald couldn't get the window lock to turn.

Margret pushed Donald aside and tried to do it herself. Nothing she did mattered, it was frozen in place.

While she was struggling with the window, the manager left only to return with a fireman who wielded a large firefighter's axe.

The fireman said, "Stand back and I'll knock this glass out and help you crawl out."

He then proceeded to bust the glass and rake the inside of the frame to reduce the sharp edges. He placed a blanket over the bottom edge and motioned for them to climb through.

Donald made it out first before turning to help Margret. She put one platformed pump out the window at a time. Then with Donald's help, she shimmied through the narrow opening.

*   *   *

Eric had been on time, but couldn't wait around while the manager tried to get the door unlocked. So, he left promising to return. He arrived again at 6:40 AM driving the company transport truck with the men inside. Cheery hellos on clean faces greeted Margret and Donald as they climbed into the back of the truck for the second time. They had already bought the part and enough antifreeze to fill the one and a half gallon radiator of the little truck. Without wasting time they only briefly stopped at the local McDonalds for a takeout breakfast.

Inside the truck, they passed the food around, everyone getting their share, and in no time Donald and Margret were back at Frank Wiseman's truck. The men replaced the hose and even filled the radiator. Then they said their goodbyes. With another delay behind them, Margret and Donald were on their way again.

What was supposed to be a five-hour drive had turned into an eleven-hour journey. With great relief and enthusiastic expectations, they excitedly arrived in Carlsbad. They checked into the Carlsbad Howard Johnson at 9:30 AM and went straight to bed.

As for laying a foundation in their marriage built on an intimate relationship, getting some quality alone time was almost impossible. Up to this point, intimacy had been hurried, like making love in a formula car in the middle of the Indianapolis 500. It seemed the lesser god named *Exhaustion* continually played havoc with their love life. As for rest, they had finally gotten some at the La Quinta in Hobbs. They promised each other they would take Monday the 9th of July as a day for the honey part of the honeymoon. The *Do Not Disturb* sign went on the door, and for the day, they took their meals from Howard Johnson's famous room service.

CHAPTER SEVENTEEN

Delivering the Goods
July 9th, 1979
Monday
4:00 PM
At Carlsbad Caverns

The solid metal from the cab to the back double doors of Harvard's Chevy truck insured complete privacy. It could have been a delivery truck from any bakery in town, and that was the point. Looking like a delivery truck from any one of the half dozen bakeries and food services in Carlsbad was perfect camouflage. It became just another truck delivering supplies and foodstuffs at the National Park's loading dock behind the information center. He casually pulled his truck into the line of others waiting to be unloaded. The food these trucks delivered would travel seven-hundred and fifty feet underground to the caverns' lunchroom in elevator number four, the one they use as a service elevator on delivery days.

There in the subterranean café, it will be prepared and boxed into what the park called gourmet picnic-style lunches.

Cafeteria workers, employed at the National Park, worked feverishly off-loading the various delivery trucks. They were expecting a record number of guests to visit the park during the busy week after the July fourth holiday.

Harvard stuck a Deadhead bumper sticker on the back bumper of the truck. It was a way for Hinto and Mika to identify his truck and come unload it. Two park service employees, Anon Mady and Bill Kelly, headed toward Harvard's truck. Hinto stopped them and said, "You guys get the next truck, Mika and I have this one. He's a friend of ours."

Unwittingly, Anon said, "Sure thing," and headed to the next truck in line.

Hinto opened the back side-by-side doors of Harvard's truck and quickly shut them after jumping in. Inside the truck, Harvard sat beside a stainless steel serving cart covered with a white linen tablecloth identical to the ones used in the underground cafeteria. On top of the cart were various boxes labeled *Hard Salami dall'Italia* and *Beef Pastrami, a product of the USA.*

Mika pulled the white cloth back, there inside the serving cart was what looked like tablecloths rolled into a bundle. Tucked inside the roll of fabric were the assault rifles. Mika unrolled the cloth and laid the guns on top of the cart. Harvard handed him box after box of the specialty ammunition. They stacked the boxes of bullets inside a larger cardboard carton labeled *Pepperoni dall'Italia* and taped it shut. Hinto drew a big red X on every side of the box. Mika busied himself by loading each rifle's clip. When the guns were prepped to his satisfaction, he rolled the guns back into the fabric bundle, added the ammunition box to the cold cut boxes and stashed the cloth bundle inside the cart. Once done they added stacks of towels, paper napkins, and paper tray mats. It was a natural camouflage for a restaurant.

At the service entrance in the Guest Information Center a United States Park Police officer, known as a USPP officer, sat half attentively protecting the park's back door. The National Park Rangers, NPR's, and the USPP worked together to ensure the safety at parks like Carlsbad Caverns. NPRs are badge carrying law enforcement officers who may or may not carry a firearm. Since 1977 even part-time NPRs must pass fire-arms certification courses. In contrast, USPP officers always carry and usually have a 9mm handgun if not another smaller gun in an ankle holster. This armed guard could be a problem.

Harvard said, "Well, it's showtime boys. Be calm and natural. That park version of a mall cop won't even look twice at the cart unless you act suspicious."

"No problem, Boss," Mika said. "We got this."

Hinto wiped the sweat off his palms onto the flimsy white food smock he wore over his black coat. "Like he said, Boss. We got this." He didn't sound convincing.

Harvard ordered, "Hinto, you stay back and take another cart in. Let Mika roll this one in through the security door." Hinto nodded his approval with a certain amount of relief.

He opened the back doors for his men. Hinto and Mika unloaded the cart from the truck. Mika headed straight for the service entrance while Hinto went to another truck. It would be easy enough to find another cart full of supplies to bring in.

With everything ready, Harvard drove the truck out of the loading zone and back to Carlsbad. If things went bad he didn't want to be around for what would happen next.

Mika coolly walked over to the service entrance guarded by the USPP officer. Behind that door and down the hall was elevator number four, used on delivery days as a service elevator. Lunchroom staff, who were unloading the trucks, lined up waiting their turn to take it all down, one load at a time, to the subterranean freezers and food storage lockers.

As usual, during the bi-weekly food deliveries, the security personnel turned the metal detector off. Today, it was useless as every load was carried in by either a stainless steel cart or a metal dolly. The guard held a clipboard marking off the number of boxes and items expected. Various paper goods, lunchmeats, bread, lettuce, tomatoes, cheese, and condiments were some of the expected items. The guard checked his list for the proper commodity and nodded his approval. Mika didn't flinch as the USPP officer looked over his cart.

Behind him, Hinto poured sweat just watching Mika take the guns through the checkpoint. He seemed excessively nervous and the guard noticed.

The USPP officer said, "You there. Stop. Roll your cart over here." Mika froze. He turned to see the guard talking to Hinto, pulling him aside, and searching his cart.

Mika hurried on through the checkpoint and down the hall to the elevator where he had to wait his turn to use elevator number four, and take the plunge down seven-hundred and fifty feet.

After searching every box stacked on Hinto's cart, and finding nothing out of the ordinary, the guard allowed Hinto to pass.

Once at the bottom of the caverns, Mika and Hinto hid the guns inside one of the stainless steel serving stations which lined the entrance of the lunchroom. Mika pulled the rolled fabric and pepperoni box from the cart, stacking them in the bin at Hinto's station. It was the closest station to the lunchroom's entrance.

The eatery had been outfitted with every foodservice convenience, as well as, a concrete floor, and a series of electrically operated freestanding stainless steel serving areas providing workspaces where employees could stand while serving the guests.

The so-called Carlsbad Caverns' luncheon room, located at end of the tour, had been installed in 1928 and remodeled to add the gift shop and information counter in the 50s. It reflected both time periods with its natural deco lines and cool atomic modernistic design. Housed in a cavern annexed adjacently to what the park rangers called the *Big Room*, the elevator's doors opened to the lunchroom, over seven hundred feet under the surface. Without the electric cables, traveling down the elevator shaft which provided power for the lights, the whole caverns would have been black as midnight, even in midday.

The day-tripping spelunkers lined up, and pushed their trays over stainless steel rails, as they selected from a variety of sandwiches, snack foods, and fruits to assemble into their lunch boxes. At the next station, they would also select the beverage of their choice. Eventually, they would reach the cashier where they would pay for their food and then sit in a large ultra-modern area to converse and enjoy the delicacies they had chosen. Round, conical fixtures jutting up from the concrete floor provided indirect lighting for the workers and park guests alike. The only parts of the room even resembling a cave were the ceiling and walls. Everything else in the lunchroom was modern and shiny.

Mika kept repeating to himself what Harvard told his men, *People don't see what's right in front of them. They see what they want to see.* He was right, of course. So, when the guests looked around in the elegantly styled restaurant, they would see nothing out of the ordinary.

The evening went as usual. Typically, exhausted and hungry people finished their tours and filed through the lunchroom line. The multitude of guests consumed a mountain of potato salad, a freezer full of cold cuts, and a river of soft drinks.

Just knowing the guns were stowed away in the undershelves made Hinto nervous, and Mika fastidiously checked his watch, repeatedly. For him time seemed to slow to a standstill, the seconds weighing heavily on the minute hand of the clock as it barely moved. Still, the one thing everyone, even Mika and Hinto, could depend on was that time would be a slave to no man, and so, eventually, it was

7:30 PM. The silent signal for the staff to start packing the leftovers in the freezer, remove the ice from under the cold cuts, empty the salad dressing canisters on the prepackaged salad buffet line, and clean their stainless steel serving stations.

The checkers were running the day's tally and the line workers were wiping the stainless steel counters to a mirror shine. Then like an automated machine at 7:45 the employees dropped everything in its proper place and headed to the elevators. It took several elevator rides before all the employees were out of the caverns and on their way home for the evening. Down seven-hundred and fifty feet below the information center in the lunchroom, the lights went dark and the USPP security guard roped off the path leading to the lunchroom. Little did they know their vigil of keeping guard over the equipment in the lunchroom also provided security for Harvard's little arsenal of AK-74s. The US Park Police of the National Parks Service were unwittingly aiding and abetting terrorists.

CHAPTER EIGHTEEN

The Cave of Wonder
July 10th, 1979
Tuesday
8:00 AM
Carlsbad, New Mexico

It was sightseeing day. Donald and Margret were up early and out of the room by 9:00 AM. They took their time meandering through the multilevel hotel and ending up in the magnificent Howard Johnson restaurant for breakfast. The Hotel's reputation had not served it justice. It was better than Margret expected. After finishing her meal she took time to fill out a costumer inquiry card commending the service and the food as both were excellent.

Margret sighed as she mentally put the past few days behind her. "Donald, I'm so glad to finally be here. This is going to be a fabulous honeymoon. Who wants to stand around in freezing temperatures looking at some old waterfall when they can go into the cave of wonders?"

"I wouldn't know Dear, I've never seen Niagara Falls, but lots of honeymooners go there, you know." He heaped a fork full of eggs Benedict on his fork and stuffed it in his mouth. After he swallowed he said. "And Darling, it's July, the temperatures at Niagara Falls isn't freezing in July."

"Who cares, after all? All I can say is it's way up north, and I'm sure a southern girl like me would freeze even in July."

He quizzically raised one eyebrow. "Oh? Whatever you say, Dear."

"I'm so excited. It's going to be exactly like seeing Aladdin's magic cave. Without the forty thieves, of course."

Donald mumbled, "And, without the gold coins, the lamp, and the genie."

"Honey, what was that you said?"

"I said can hardly wait to get going and see the scenery."

"When do we get there, to the caverns I mean?"

"If I remember right, it takes about forty to fifty minutes to drive there from the hotel."

"That long? I was wanting to get there right away."

"Nope. It's out in the middle of nowhere. You can't see anything but mesquite trees, cactus, and sand lizards. Then we'll drive up to an enormous parking lot and a couple of isolated buildings. That's the *Guest Information Center* and the *Park Offices*, I think. I can't remember exactly what the buildings are called, but even from there you can't see anything even resembling a cave."

Margret said, "Hurry and finish your breakfast, Dear. The faster we get there, the faster we get to see the sights." Then she rummaged through her beach ball sized purse until she found a small box. She handed it to Donald.

He looked puzzled. "What's this? A wedding gift?"

"Don't be silly, Donald. It's your boutonnière."

He tossed it on the café-table. "Okay, and what do I want it for?"

"I want you to wear it on your collar, silly."

Donald grimaced and opened the box. "Whatever you say, Margret." He kept fumbling and fussing with the pin in the boutonnière. "Why do I have to wear this stupid flower on my shirt? I'll look ridiculous, and the pin keeps sticking me."

"I insist you wear it. It's a reminder of our love for each other,"

"I thought that was what the rings were for."

"My daddy paid good money for the flowers, and I want to get *his* money's worth out of them."

Donald gritted his teeth, then politely said, "Yes, dear, but do I have to get *his* money's worth by wearing the stupid thing?"

"Just for today sweetie... please," She sweetly replied as she pushed her bottom lip forward. "It will wither soon."

Donald muttered under his breath, "Not soon enough for me."

"What was that, Dear?"

"We can't get there fast enough for me," he replied. He wasn't exactly sure why, but she was starting to sound as demanding as his mother.

"Well, if we get there and get the sightseeing over with, we'll be back in our room early."

Spiritedly Donald added, "Then we can put a little more honey on our honeymoon."

"Dear, after walking all day I'm sure I'll have a headache." She looked over at him, smiled and said, "from the waist down, at least."

Not knowing what to say after that, Donald finished his breakfast in silence.

*   *   *

On the way to the caverns, Donald was glad his father's truck had a good air conditioner. The mercury had climbed up over a hundred degrees and it wasn't even noon, yet. Already waves of heat radiated off of the black asphalt.

They headed down the winding two-way leading to the caverns. The drive would take another twenty minutes, and then they would have to wait in line at the information center for their tour guide to assemble enough people to start.

For their first time at the caverns, Margret and Donald decided to get the full experience and opted for the long walk through all the nooks and crannies as they leisurely meandered their way down. This walk would take most of the day. They expected to reach the *Big Room* about 3:00 PM. They would be hungry and tired from the full-fledged excursion, and ready for a late lunch.

The guide introduced herself to the park guests as Park Ranger Sarah, and she soon called out, "The eleven o'clock long tour is starting now. All interested in doing the long walking tour follow me. Those wanting the short walking tour wait here. It will start in thirty minutes."

Sarah stopped the group in front of what looked like a crack in the earth. Margret asked, "Is that the cave entrance?"

Donald replied, "Yep. Looks like God took an ax and opened a space in the ground, right?"

"I don't know what I was expecting, but it certainly wasn't this." Disappointed, she looked at the rough terrain surrounding the open fissure shaped chasm and sighed. "Thanks to whomever it was who came up with the idea of putting paved trails over to the cave." She suddenly looked down reappraising her clothes. "I should have asked if I was dressed okay for spelunking. What do you think?"

Donald inspected her with a glance. She stood there tilting one foot like a fashion model, and wearing a pair of white gabardine bell bottoms and a navy blue, nautical style, crop top.

He replied, "Yeah, if there's a flood in the caverns, you'll be able to sail us out on the lost ship of the desert."

"Donald Wiseman, you can be insufferable sometimes." Half in jest she swatted his cheek with her freshly laundered and pressed handkerchief.

He laughed. "It's a gift, honestly. It just comes natural."

She tucked the handkerchief in the top of her slacks and asked, "Does the asphalt walkway go all the way through the cave or do we have to climb?"

Donald stood looking over a cave map in one of the official handouts he'd picked up at the information center. "No climbing. There's a few steps but the walkway goes all the way through. I can't say it's straight or level, but it goes all the way to where the lunchroom and the elevators are. Thankfully they await to bring us back to the surface."

"What's the fun in that? I'm sure we'll want to walk the path back out."

She reached out her hand for Donald to take. He didn't notice. He was busy reading the brochure.

"Donald! Take my hand," she snapped. He did, and she cooed, "There, all better. I might need a little help if I lose my balance on one of these winding pathways," and without delay, they followed the tour guide into the cave.

In the area just past the natural entrance and before a steep drop was a space the guide called an outer cave; there, hundreds of thousands of bats clung to the ceiling of the cavern. In the half-darkness, they were barely recognizable as bats. If it were not for their soft squeals and eerie cries and the immense amount of guano, a visitor might not notice them. After Park Ranger Sarah pointed them out the first time guests gasped in horror.

Margret stepped delicately trying to not get bat guano on her favorite platform espadrilles. Her efforts were futile. There was too much guano, and her shoes would carry the odious souvenir with them down the path.

The guide explained, "The bats only live at the cave opening. The farther we go into the cave, their population dwindles to zero."

As Donald promised, an asphalt walkway for the fair-weather spelunkers made it easy to walk through the entire cave. When the way became extra steep, the National Parks Service had thoughtfully provided handrails on which they could lean and cling to.

From her backpack, the tour guide handed out cellophane packaged earphones. They were made of cheap plastic and foam rubber. She said, "Unwrap your headsets and give the wrappers to me. I'll dispose of them later."

Margret asked, "Donny, what are these for? Are we going to listen to music as we walk?"

He shrugged and replied, "This is new. They didn't have this when I was here before."

The tour guide stuffed the clear plastic wrappings in her backpack. "Here in the depth of darkness we have brought civilization to your fingertips, but you have no idea what I'm talking about." She laughed and said, "I'm sure you all are tired of my rambling on about the various stalactites and stalagmites. From here through the Big Room at the end of our tour, the marked attractions have been brought into the twentieth century with the miracle of radio broadcasting. Using the marvel of something called transistors makes it possible to hide a miniaturized transmitter, emitting a weak radio signal, behind each marker."

Before continuing her explanation, she handed out little rectangular boxes, the size of transistor radios, with a miniature headphone jack in the top and a clip on the back. "I'll collect these from you in the lunchroom. If I miss you, please return them to the Information Center before you leave the park."

She made sure everyone clipped the radios onto their clothing and placed the headphone jacks into the top socket. "Now, surely you're wondering how this works. Just follow me."

She instructed the group to walk toward an exhibit marker. "It's quite simple and ingenious. As you approach a marker, you will hear information about the exhibit in your earphones." Park Ranger Sarah announced, "Please stay on the path where hidden electric lights will illuminate our way. Of course, I will walk with you, and if you have questions about the cave, feel free to ask. But, most of your questions will be answered by the automated guide in your headsets."

The tour group walked on past a series of steep switchbacks leading down into the bowels of the earth. They walked for hours exploring the cave along the provided pathway. Several paths led to areas marked restricted, keep out. As no one had any desire to get lost or thrown out of the cave, they stayed on the approved path.

Margret and Donald walked and listened to the automated information for about forty minutes before they reached a room called the King's Palace. The name was very fitting. The stalactites, columns, and stalagmites were crusted with tiny round knobs and covered with a thin layer of water making them sparkle like gems. It was easy to imagine this room being the throne room for the king of the fairies. Some of the guests took pictures, but even the Palace of Versailles full of gold and mirrors, couldn't match the grandeur of this the King's chamber at Carlsbad Caverns.

Margret reached over with her handkerchief and halfheartedly slapped Donald on the cheek with it. "You let me forget the camera."

"Sorry, Sweetie, We left in such a hurry I didn't think to get it."

The Queens Chamber, a cave adjacent to the King's Palace, was filled with what the tour guide called curtains. Flowing ribbons of stone covered with a thin layer of water dripping from the ceiling of the cave made them glimmer like fabrics woven with metallic threads.

"Oh, this room reminds me that we need a place to live when we get back. I hope your father is looking for us an apartment."

"Yes Dear. We can call him from the Information Center when we get back to the surface."

"I think we should plan on a three-bedroom house."

"Why? Three bedrooms are expensive and we don't need the room."

"Not now we don't... but we'll have family coming in from out of town and then eventually we will be needing a nursery."

"A nursery?" He choked the words out, making his voice sound louder than he had anticipated. "Are you sure?"

"Oh, not for now—for later."

The guests on the tour had started staring at them as they were distracted from the beauty of the cave, and distracting everyone else.

"Donald, you're getting loud. People are staring," said Margret.

"Yes, Dear," he whispered.

The exploration in those rooms alone took almost an hour. Then it was back to traversing down along the pathway listening to the headphones. After three and a half hours of electronic guided exploration, Margret and Donald's group made it through the *Big Room*. It was seven minutes after three o'clock.

The air was chilly, almost cold In the *Big Room*. Margret shivered and said, "I should have brought a sweater, but   who would have thought I'd need it in July when it's a hundred and two degrees in the desert."

"I'm sorry," Donald apologetically replied. "I should have warned you about the temperature change underground."

The automated guide, unaffected by the chilly air, kept talking about one rock formation after another. Park Ranger, Sarah, announced, "If you're hungry there's a lunchroom to your left where you may buy your lunch. There's also a gift shop where you can purchase souvenirs of your trip. Once you've eaten, you may want to walk back up to the surface or you may decide to ride the elevator up. For those who want to walk, I will be making the return trip in one hour. That should give everyone time to eat and browse the gift shop." It was a memorized speech which she recited dutifully at the halfway point of her daily hike.

Margret rubbed her aching calves and said, "I can't imagine having a job requiring so much walking. She must have leg muscles like an Olympic athlete."

"I certainly don't want her job, thank you," Donald confessed. "I'm happy tending to my Heidelberg offset press back at the printing company. No one comes by to thank me for what I do, and I don't have to hike a hundred miles every day to the center of the Earth." He glanced over at the lunchroom. "I'm starving. Let's see what trolls and under-dwellers have for lunch." With hunger motivating them, Margret and Donald went straight for the lunchroom.

Margret selected ham and cheese on rye from a swarthy foodservice worker wearing a long black coat under his white foodservice smock. The nameplate pinned to his smock identified him as *Hinto*.

He kept looking at his watch, and at length said, "Excuse me. It's 3:20 and I have a scheduled break. I'll be right back." He put a closed sign on his serving line and walked over to three men standing nearby.

CHAPTER NINTEEN

Four Corners of an Oval Room
July 10th, 1979
Tuesday
3:25 PM
The Lunchroom at Carlsbad Caverns

There were two ways to get in or out of the lunchroom. One way was to walk back up through the caverns. The second was to take one of the four high-speed elevators. One in which the food had been delivered underground. This route only took seconds and left the passengers with an unnatural queasy feeling.

Mika felt sick to his stomach, but it had nothing to do with the elevator. His nerves were frayed as he hunkered behind Hinto's serving station handing out the AK-74s to Harvard and the men. Hinto kept checking his watch and looking over at him. The four novice terrorists were about to make their move.

Mika said the words he knew Hinto needed to hear. "Bro, keep it cool and nothing will go wrong. Harvard knows what he's doing. He won't let us down. You'll see. Be tough and stand strong."

*   *   *

After going through the food line, Margret and Donald took their sandwiches to the seating area where they were relaxing from the excessive walking. The three men who Margret saw Hinto talking to suddenly stood up from behind one of the service counters and opened fire. The repetitive blasts from the automatic weapons sounded like raging claps of thunder as they fired streams of bullets into the caverns' ceiling, causing a rain of dust to fall into the Big Room. To Donald and Margret the automatic assault rifles looked like small cannons. The terrorists fired again, forcing the guests to cluster into groups.

"Back up," Hinto yelled. "I said back the fuck up, you gringo yuppies." He wildly shot over the heads of the tourists chipping hunks of rock out of the cave wall. The sound was deafening as it echoed through the cave.

Margret screamed in terror as Donald grabbed her by the waist, pulling her back to the wall of the lunchroom.

A USPP officer serving as a security guard pulled his gun on Hinto and yelled, "Put your weapon down!" In a synchronized motion, Mika slapped him with the butt of his AK-74 knocking the officer to the ground. Hinto then grabbed the revolver and kicked the guard.

"Stand up fool. Stand up or I'll kick your shitty brains out of your shitty head."

The officer managed to stand as Hinto pushed him and the tourists into a tight group.

Harvard had disarmed the only other USPP officer who doubled as a security guard. The required firearms training for USPP made them well versed in the use of their firearm, but they were not trained or prepared to repel this kind of tactical invasion. The terrorists had taken the park police and park rangers by complete surprise.

Harvard yelled, "The odds are some of you palefaces have weapons. Here's how this is going to go. My friend Tarby here is going to walk around with a bag. You put your knife or gun into the bag. If you shoot my friend, I'll shoot one of these pretty ladies in the tour group. If you keep your gun and I find it later, I'll shoot one of the pretty ladies. If you keep your gun and shoot me, my friends will shoot as many pretty ladies as they can."

Tarby started collecting knives and a couple of guns. By chance, they had kidnapped not only helpless tourists but a couple of off duty cops, too. Surrender of their weapons came only from remorse at the thought of them being the cause of someone's death, and by surrendering their weapon it resulted in a potentially more lethal situation than before. For not only did the terrorists have the impressive assault rifles, but also a stash of four handguns collected from the off duty officers and the USPP guards.

Fear flooded Margret's eyes with tears as she looked at Donald. She was panic-stricken, her blood felt cold, and she couldn't move—petrified by fear into a silent state of shock. No words could express the sheer terror raging across her face. The honeymooners were herded into Hinto's group of hostages. In an automatic motion, Margret pulled Donald down to the floor by her. They huddled together near a table.

She asked, "What do we do now?"

"Pray."

They stood and leaned toward each other as she put her head on his shoulder. Leaning on him with her eyes closed, she appeared to be praying, but the voice in her head screamed in silence.

Hinto heard them talking and shot toward her feet, the bullets chewing up the concrete only yards in front of her, throwing fragments up at her like splinters.

"Did that catch your attention, Honey? Shut the hell up or the next round goes through your head."

Donald stepped in front of her to stand on the gaping bullet chipped concrete. "Leave her alone!"

By the time Donald managed to step between her and the gunman, panic and fear had brought Margret to the point of collapse. She stumbled, went limp, and started falling.

Donald turned, just in time, to catch his fainting bride. He managed to sit her beside him and hold her tightly. Quietly and calmly he whispered in her ear. "I'm here with you. We can make it through this. You've got to pull yourself together."

She stirred. Whispering she asked, "Why are they doing this? Are they insane?"

"Money, Darling—the only reason I can think of is money. We'll do exactly what these guys tell us to, then they'll get their money, and we'll all go home."

"But, Donald, we don't have any money. Not much anyway."

"It's ransom their after. We've been kidnapped."

Bewilderment overcame her terror as she realized their whole tour group, as well as, the food service workers and the guard were being held hostage.

Harvard yelled, "Men take a corner." Simultaneously the terrorists divided the hostages into four groups and forced them into different parts of the irregular-shaped room.

Tarby had followed Harvard's lead and had herded his hostages into a tight circle, forcing them over to his corner of the lunchroom. In due course, all four corners of the odd-shaped underground cafe were inhabited by crowded panic-stricken captives.

The melee had traumatized the spelunking tourists into a tribe of obedient puppets, moving only at their master's command. In a planned attempt to psychologically intimidate the hostages the terrorists hit several of the larger men with the butt of their guns, humiliating them, forcing them to comply with their demeaning commands.

Mika was harassing a particularly big man. On any ordinary day, this mountain of a man would have broken little Mika into pieces. He slapped the man across the side of his head. His ear was starting to bleed. "There, you big son of a bitch, take that. How's it feel being one of the little guys? Huh? Your mama's not going to come help you now."

Harvard yelled, "Stop plan beta. Enough of the fun shit, start deployment of plan gamma."

To the trained off duty policemen in the crowd, the use of the terms *alpha, beta, gamma,* and *delta* indicated an extensive organization was involved in the kidnapping, and the powerful automatic rifles spoke volumes about the professionalism of the hijackers.

One of the four, the loud one they called Harvard, was clearly in charge. Like an orchestra leader commanding his musicians to play in unison this man called the shots, and together the terrorists' worked like the concomitantly harmonious movement of a well-trained chorus. Harvard returned to the center of the room, turned and shot a line into the concrete floor spraying his captives with sharp slivers of rock and cement. He yelled at his corner section and warned them to not step across the line or else he would blow their brains all over the cave wall.

Every hostage recoiled from the line as if it were a venomous snake. With assurance he had the terrified ensemble under his control, Harvard returned to the center of the lunchroom. From there he yelled instructions to the other three terrorists.

When prudence eventually overcame terror and comprehension settled in, Donald realized they were prisoners in a seven hundred and fifty-foot pit, held hostage by terrorists who were using military-style tactics and powerful automatic assault rifles.

A terrorist, the one Margret had identified as Hinto, grabbed the off duty cops and the USPP officer who pulled the gun. Forcing them, at gunpoint, up against an elevator's doors, he said, "You're going up this elevator and tell the idiots up there to get us a million bucks and an airplane to take us to Brazil."

With his AK-74 slung over one shoulder, Harvard held the captured guard's revolver, point blank, to the back of Hinto's head. "Shut the fuck up," Harvard told Hinto. "I do the talking. From now till this is over, I call every fuckin' shot, and if you forget again, I'll blow your fucking brains out. Got that?"

With a disgusted look on his face, Hinto stepped away. Harvard wasn't satisfied with Hinto's attitude. He spat on the ground and repeated, "Only I talk—you got it?"

Hinto nodded.

Harvard un-cocked the pistol and lowered it to his side. "Now, get to the plan like we practiced it."

Hinto's over-enthusiasm and machismo indirectly challenged his leadership, and he had promised to kill anyone who tried to take charge, but he needed these guys a little longer. He had to prove himself to his men, and take the lead again.

In a gesture of recompense, Harvard said, "Bro, I brought some liquid courage with me. Thought we all might need a little before this is done." He reached into his coat and pulled out a small flask. Handing it to Hinto, he said, "Calm yourself. Share it with Tarby and Mika. We're only getting started."

Harvard turned and grabbed one of the rangers and hit him. Blood oozed from the corner of the guard's mouth. In a calm and calculated manner the loud leader of the terrorists faced the men standing in front of the elevators and said, "As you see, we mean business. I've estimated about a hundred hostages we've taken. You're going upstairs like Hinto said, and you're going to tell your bosses we want four million dollars, and to be air-lifted to the Jicarilla Apache Indian Reservation north of Los Alamos. Those are our demands, and we want it by sundown or the hostages die one at a time. You have five hours. That's all. Tell them Mika Loadstar, Hinto Hawk, and Tarby Thompson said after sundown the fate of these palefaces are on your shoulders. That's when I start executing them one every thirty minutes. It'll be your fault. Got it?" The men nodded and headed straight into the elevator. The metal doors closed, and they ascended straight to the surface.

Mika said, "Boss, you just gave the feds our names. Why?"

"I'm making you famous boys. That's all, just making you famous."

As planned, Tarby had his hostages move the restaurant furniture into a barricade, filling the open walkway leading into the *Big Room.* They also stacked pieces of various movable restaurant equipment onto the center of the asphalt path.

Margret, who had been fairly calm after waking from her fainting spell, became overly excited again when Hinto started shooting over their heads forcing them to protect themselves from falling debris with their hands and crouch into a sitting position.

Mika put his hand on Hinto's shoulder and asked, "You feel better, Bro?"

Hinto answered, "Hell yeah."

He took a swig from Harvard's flask and gave it to Mika. "Here, Harvard gave me this to pass around. Called it liquid courage. It works pretty well. I've only had two drinks and I'm feeling better already."

Mika sipped it at first, but the flask was small, and it didn't take much to drain it.

Margret sat trying not to hyperventilate, gasping for air, trying to control the onset of another panic attack.

"Stay calm and stay close to me," Donald pleaded.

With her breathing moderately under control, she said, "As much as I'd like to make plans to start back to the motel. Something tells me that's not happening anytime soon."

To her left Park Ranger Sarah sat holding her ankles and muttering a prayer.

"Has this ever happened before? I mean, do you guys have some kind of protocol for this kind of thing?" Margret asked.

Park Ranger Sarah shook her head as she spoke, "Never. This has never happened before."

Weakly Margret asked, "Do you think they'll kill us?"

"No, I don't think they took us hostage to massacre us. That doesn't mean they won't make an example of one or two." She cleared her throat and continued, "Being a park ranger, I'm the most likely to be chosen when it comes time."

Margret took her hand. "You're not dead, yet."

"No, but they could literally mow down this whole corner full of hostages with one of those assault rifles."

"What worries me," Margret said. "If they get what they want, they could still slaughter us all."

Donald then spoke up saying, "Not likely, Darling. When the FBI gets here, and I'm sure they're on their way, they'll take command of this situation. If they kill us all, then the FBI will charge in with guns blazing, and the terrorists will have lost their leverage."

Margret looked up at the ceiling of the cave. "Dear God in heaven... My worst imagined fears come true. So, you're telling me the bright side is if we're all dead, it gives the FBI a chance to catch these creeps." She rolled her eyes. "Oh Lord, then we're all done for. What good will that do?"

"No, Dearest, they aren't going to rush in guns blazing." He sighed and whispered, "At least, I don't think they will."

Each corner had a line shot into the concrete like an invisible fence, daring the huddling captives to step past it. Two gunmen stood back-to-back in the center of the lunchroom. A third terrorist watched the lunchroom's barricaded entrance while the loud one, Harvard, walked around in silence giving commands to his men in gestures and signals.

Margret was trying to be brave. She couldn't even look at poor Park Ranger Sarah for fear they might shoot her as an example of their authority. Sitting in silence, Margret placidly watched the terrorists as expressionless tears flowed down her cheeks. Her emotions were out of control. No one could have prophesied this at her wedding. Margret sobbed in an expressionless trance. After some time, Donald managed to get through her semi-catatonic shock, and they held each other waiting to see what would come next. She buried her head into Donald's chest. All her weeping turned his shirt into a wet soggy mess. Her tears had turned into dry sobs.

Powerless and fully aware of his impotence, Donald patted her on the head, stroked her hair, and said, "There, There... it's all going to turn out all right. I promise." His inner voice said something else. *How can I make such an absurdly impossible promise? I suppose if my words make her feel better, it's something.* Without a doubt, their situation looked near hopeless. *Surely, she sees through my false bravado.* He knew he was as helpless as she.

CHAPTER TWENTY

Proof of Life
July 10th, 1979
Tuesday
4:00 PM
At Carlsbad Caverns National Park

The park rangers were the first on the scene, and the ranger delegated to the job of negotiating had only one previous experience.

On that occasion, this novice negotiator had successfully separated a child from an armed father, a divorced parent, who the mother accused of kidnapping because he had taken his son out of the state to visit the caverns for a weekend. The only similarity between these events was the presence of a gun. As different as that was from this fiasco, there were certain advantages he had at the time. Even then, he had been able to make visual assessments of the situation. Visual cues made it easy to ascertain what the gunman was thinking, and what his intentions were. That had been over in a few minutes, but this was different.

With tons of rock between him and the terrorists, he was blind to their actions. He relied completely on the intelligence gathered from the statements of the released officers and the ranger.

He needed to bide his time and wait for a more experienced hostage negotiator to arrive. He understood how critical communication was, and so, the novice negotiator was also taking advantage of the intercom as a clandestine listening device. It proved to be the perfect eavesdropping tool because it could be set to listen to conversations in the lunchroom, even when it wasn't being used as a two-way radio. The terrorist's leader chose to talk over the cave's intercom to the novice negotiator in the information center.

As state of the art as the intercom was, it didn't help when the terrorists were silent. The problem was there wasn't any distinctive chatter from the terrorists. The only one yelling out orders was their loud leader, and he had fallen silent. The only sound the park ranger could hear was the mutterings of the hundred kidnapped hostages. One grumbling hostage would make a discernible sound, but with a hundred frightened prisoners corralled into a tight space, their sounds would become confused mutterings and completely indistinguishable voices—and so it was with the hostages.

Dazed by the terror and all but delirious, Margret whispered, "Donald, I was thinking,"

"Yes, Babe," Donald replied. "What are you thinking?" He was just chattering as if his words could get her mind off the danger surrounding them.

"These people are from everywhere on Earth. They've traveled hundreds, and some of them came thousands, of miles to be here right now. They spent hard-earned money to be kidnapped by these criminals."

"I suppose they did. They had no idea they were paying for such an exciting adventure."

"Is this what you call an exciting adventure?"

"Well, Honey, what else would you call it?"

"Torture. I think I'd call it torture."

"You know, there's a bright side."

"Oh? And, don't say it's being shot." She looked up at him, "Pray tell, what's the bright side?"

"This trip can't get any worse."

She looked at him from the side of her eyes and said, "Donald, don't count on it. This honeymoon isn't over yet."

He tried to sound reassuring, "Do what they ask, but stay in the group, and try to be invisible. We'll get out of this yet. You'll see."

Shivering with fear and whispering, Margret repeated the only thought forcing its way to her consciousness, "Donny, what are we going to do? ... what are we doing?"

"Sweetie, just pray for a miracle."

Hinto Hawk yelled at them, "You, there."

Donald raised his eyebrows and pointed at himself.

Hinto yelled, "Yes, you with the pansy flower pinned to your shirt."

He wanted to be sarcastic. An *I told you so* would have fit in perfectly. *It's that damned flower. It caught their attention. I knew I shouldn't have worn it.* But, instead, Donald politely replied, "It's not a pansy it's a carnation." Without hesitation, Hinto slapped him with the butt of the rifle.

"I said, Shut the hell up. You and Miss Sailor Lady have been chattin' like gossipin' hens. Don't you understand when I say, shut the hell up?"

Donald didn't reply he held his throbbing head and nodded the best he could.

Harvard looked over at Hinto and asked, "Did you say one of these guys is wearing a carnation on his shirt?"

Hinto whispered back. "Yeah. This freak with the lady sailor. That's what he said it was—a carnation. Bro, you want me to make an example of him to show the feds we mean business?"

"No. I want him and Suzy Sailor there to join my group. Take two out of the group in my corner and switch them out for those two nautical niceties. He's the one I've been looking for."

"Boss, you know this guy?" Hinto asked.

Harvard said, "Don't ask a stupid question. Don't be a *pendejo*, be *inteligente*. Of course, I don't know him, but I've met hundreds of people just like him."

Hinto retaliated, "Dude, speak English. I don't speak Spanish."

Hinto grabbed Donald by the collar, and almost choking him, pulled him to his feet. Margret stood up holding on to his shirttail as Hinto all but dragged her husband to Harvard's corner.

"Stop. You're hurting him!" She yelled.

167

He all but threw Donald, and subsequently Margret too, into the mass of people huddling in Harvard's corner before he ordered two of the female hostages to move to his group; then he returned to stand guard over his own designated hostages.

A quivering voice on the intercom said, "You're going to have to give us more time. Nothing like this has ever happened before. Getting four million in small bills in a burg like Carlsbad isn't as easy as it might be in a big city like El Paso... and we don't have an international airport, loaded with big helicopters, neither. You'll have to do with a little chopper."

"You don't have any leverage here. We have all the cards." Harvard announced, "Before you even knew we were here, we set IEDs and remote-controlled charges along the path outside the lunchroom. If anyone tries to approach us from the cave entrance we detonate the charges from in here by radio remote control, and your precious *Wonder of the Natural World* rumbles and collapses taking a hundred souls to hell with it. Keep everyone away from the paths leading to the lunchroom, understand?"

Harvard had four aces up his sleeve. It was time to play one. He demanded, "I want to talk to someone in the media—a television reporter. I need to do an interview. What I have to say can only be said to the press and in person. It's got to be a big shot, you hear me? You send down someone I've never heard of, and I'll start killing hostages." His thoughts were focused on not showing his hand all at once.

Timing was important. He had to play his cards at the right time, and he had just played his first ace.

"Yes. I'll do my best to find someone who can interview you. As for your safety... I assure you, no one is trying to sneak up on you. I promise." He paused, then said, "We're taking no chances with the lives of the hostages."

"Good, because we're watching. We're ready to die here, and personally introduce these innocent souls to Satan. Those are our demands, and if they're not met every soul down here will pay the price." Then the com fell silent. The rookie negotiator wondered if the reoccurring reference to hell meant they thought of themselves as demons, or perhaps they felt closer to the center of the Earth where he believed hell was located. One thing was for sure, this Harvard was smart, probably college-educated. He didn't curse profanely like the others and he articulated his demands in precise English.

"I need to talk to one of the hostages to be sure they're still alive." He was trying to do everything by the book, and after all the gunfire, the first thing his supervisor would want to know was if he had proof of life.

Harvard grabbed Margret by the arm and pulled her to a standing position. Donald stood with her and threw an ineffective punch, missing Harvard, but swishing a lot of air. Harvard whipped the butt end of his gun around smacking Donald squarely in the forehead, knocking him out. Harvard dragged Margret over to the microphone. "Sweet-cheeks, talk to the man. He wants to know if I killed anyone yet."

Margret could hardly talk. All she could manage was a mumble, "I'm all right. We're all alive. At least for the moment. Please get us out of here."

The negotiating park ranger said, "Stay calm. We're doing our best here. We hope they will see how completely useless it is to continue this prank."

Harvard took the microphone, and let go of Margret who rushed back to Donald's side. "This is no prank. Didn't the guard I sent up tell you? We're armed with the new automatic AK-74 Assault Rifles and we have enough ammunition, food, and water to survive a month-long siege. Although, I doubt the hostages will last that long."

Margret took her linen handkerchief, wiped the dirt from Donald's unconscious face, and held him tight. Her hero laid in her arms, knocked senseless by the brutality of a terrorist. She knew Donald had never been one for conflict, but he was willing to charge in where angels feared to tread, all for her. What else could she ask for in a husband? He slowly stirred as they sat on the cold concrete floor.

Harvard listened to the voice on the intercom as it said, "I believe you. We're taking this threat seriously. We're working on your demands, have a little patience."

The truth was, Harvard had planned his every word. He was intentionally putting the negotiator at the disadvantage by not allowing the park ranger to converse with him more than necessary. He yelled into the mic, "When you have the money, we'll talk more. Until then, keep quiet." He paused then spit out the words, "You hear me, I'm not listening to any of your shit."

The intercom fell silent.

Donald had regained his senses. "Margret, are you okay? Did that monster hurt you?"

Her fear had somehow subsided. She began whispering to not draw unwanted attention. "No. I'm fine. All they needed me for was to talk to the official on the surface, and confirm we're not all dead. For all the authorities knew, these bloodthirsty terrorists could have killed half of us already."

"I failed you. I'm not the man you think I am. I'm not macho like Marcus and Tommy."

"They're not brave," she replied, "they're stupid, and wouldn't know what to do when a thug grabbed their girl." She actually laughed. It was a pleasant thing for Donald to hear. She continued, "They'd probably faint from sheer fright." Talking about the boys was like medicine. "Those idiot brothers of mine, more than likely, would get themselves killed simply because they don't have the sense God gave a goose. They'd cross that line just to prove they could do it. And, that would be the end of them. Have no doubt, I know them better than anyone else alive. I'm telling you the God's truth, they're not as brave as they let on." She was smiling as she held Donald's head in her lap, caressing his forehead, and stroking back his hair. The spot in the center of his forehead was bright pink tinted scarlet, soon to turn dark violet. "I bet if they were in your situation, they would be shaking in their platform, blue suede, disco shoes."

The initial scare of the weapons and the shock of being kidnaped had passed, and even though Donald's head hurt he could think clearer than before. He sat up and took Margret's hand.

In a whisper, Margret cautioned, "Honey, don't get up too quickly. I'm sure you have a concussion."

"I'll be fine. I what to get where I can watch these guys." Donald was at last able to see their situation with a calmer head. He said, "They haven't killed any of us. I don't think they want to." He leaned one way and then another looking around the lunchroom at the organization of the terrorists. "From what I can tell, I think my first thought about them only wanting money was wrong. They have some agenda here. Something besides the money."

"What?" Margret asked as she looked closely for the first time at her captors.

Donald's calm attitude was like a healing balm. She managed to relax and maintain her calm. Her husband's tranquil composure combined with venting about her brothers got her mind off the peril; talking had somehow helped to release her tension and lift her brain fog of trauma and fear. With it no longer controlling her, she asked, "Why? Why then do you think they're doing this?"

"I don't know, but if I'm right, when that reporter gets here, we'll find out."

CHAPTER TWENTY-ONE

The Military Verses the FBI
July 10th, 1979
5:00 PM
Tuesday
In the Lunchroom

The intercom remained silent for an hour. That was when the military, the FBI, and first emergency medical personnel arrived. The military came on the scene in a series of five Sikorsky Black Hawk helicopters from Holloman Air Force Base. Each Black Hawk brought ten armed soldiers to the park. Only one federal chopper, a Sikorsky S-76 utility helicopter, brought in the FBI team of negotiators straight from El Paso.

Flying in had been the fastest route to the remote location. It beat the option of driving armored trucks with special weapons and tactical military vehicles down the single long winding road leading to the cave's *Guest Information Center.*

The military aircraft landed only moments before the FBI disembarked from the federal chopper. The time delay between when the terrorists took control of the cavern, and when the federal and military forces arrived gave the terrorists a huge advantage.

Colonel Henry McMillian, the Alamogordo CIC— military commander in charge— Instantly assessed the park ranger talking to the terrorists. "Son, I can tell by looking at you, you don't know your ass from a hole in the ground. What makes you think you can do this?"

The park ranger, not accountable to the Colonel's direct command, replied, "Well, Sir, I beg to differ. Here at the caverns is one place on earth where we have an awfully big hole in the ground, and my ass ain't that big."

The Colonel straightened to his full height. "You're an incompetent and an impertinent smart ass. If you were in my unit, I'd have you court-martialed. If you continue to speak to those maniacs like you've been doing, you'll have dead civilians lining the trail from here to the bottom of the cave."

The visual conjured by the Colonel's words made the park ranger shudder. He raised the mic in an act of surrender.

An elegant woman wearing what looked like a man's black suit stepped around the ranger and grabbed the microphone before the Colonel could take it.

"Actually," she said, "I believe he did quite well considering his inexperience. He got them talking and heard their demands. He shut down elevators two, three and four to keep the trouble underground, and he stationed armed rangers at elevator number one's doors. We certainly don't want them taking over the whole park."

She put a hand on the park ranger's shoulder. "From what I see, that in itself was quite a trick." She yelled to someone behind her, "Agent Hinez, put a lid on this. I don't want the name *Carlsbad* on any news channel before we make an official statement. *Zip it uptight.* No leaks. When the reporters arrive sequester them in the waiting area of the park office suite. For all I care they can wait it out in the maintenance annex, but I don't want them hovering over my shoulder."

She paused only long enough to take a breath. "And, set up our command center in the staff break room. We'll need to add lines to their phone system. So, find the phone hub and make the necessary changes. Make sure I have a direct line to FBI Director Webster. Let's get ready to shake things up."

Agent George Hinez, her second in command, yelled back, "You got it, Boss. No media coverage from this point on."

She turned to the novice negotiator. "We'll take it from here."

"Holy bells in hell," said the Colonel. "And, just who in Sam Hill are you?"

She extended her hand in a strong manly gesture and confidently replied, "FBI Negotiator Charlene Keller and these people with me are my negotiation team." She produced an FBI badge and flashed it his way. Agent Keller continued, "Colonel, until we know more about our situation, we could use your help clearing the cave of panicking sightseers."

175

The Colonel started to object. He chewed on the words he wanted to say. "What? The FBI sent you? This is gonna require someone with balls, and little lady, I don't think it's you."

She sat down next to the Ranger who'd established contact with the terrorists, crossed her legs—ankle to knee, and said, "Colonel, don't let this lipstick fool you." She looked up, meeting his eyes and holding his stare. "I have balls, big ones, and I filled my jockstrap the hard way." Her stare didn't flinch while she smiled.

He held her stare for a long moment. Finally, the Colonel huffed, "Okay Agent Keller, I'm going to give you a chance. Maybe you know what you're doing. I suppose you've been in hostage situations before and negotiated a suitable release of the hostages."

"Of course, I have. Colonel, this is not my first rodeo and according to those birds on your shoulder, I'm betting you've hosted a few, too. But, this isn't a kick-ass-and-take-names moment. This is going to take finesse, not brawn."

He huffed, "Alright then. You have today and if you can't negotiated the hostages out of there by midnight... It's my turn. I'll get them out. I guarantee it."

Turning away from Agent Keller, he nodded and returned his attention to the novice negotiator. "Son, You may be insolent, but if everything Agent Keller said about you is true, then you're a damned good ranger. My men will need guidance through the cave. They don't know the layout and you and your fellow rangers are the experts here."

"Yes sir. We can do that." The park ranger reached over and snatched up a bulky walkie-talkie. "All available park rangers meet at the cave's natural entrance by the Information Center. The military needs our help."

The Colonel grimaced. "I can't keep calling you son. What's your name?"

"My name's Ronald Bateman, but everyone here calls me Park Ranger Ron."

"Okay, Park Ranger Ron." The Colonel looked around in a meaningless gesture to emphasize his disapproval of how the situation was being handled. "Where are your USPP officers?"

"The U. S. Park Police? They're our armed forces here and have set up a no-go-zone around the lunchroom. We want to guarantee no one accidentally detonates one of the IEDs which the terrorist claimed to have set." He looked up at the Colonel who seemed bewildered. "The elevators go down to the lunchroom. It's a facility located in a small part of the cave, seven hundred-fifty feet down."

"Holy mother. That's one hell of an elevator ride," the Colonel said.

"Yes Sir, it is. Anyway, that's where the terrorists and the hostages are. As far as we can tell they've captured a hundred hostages and managed to barricade themselves into the lunchroom. The USPP officers are currently holding a perimeter containing the violence to that area."

"How do you communicate with those officers? Do you have to use some kind of cave runner to take messages back and forth?"

"A cave runner would be too slow, and we certainly can't get a walkie-talkie to broadcast that far even if there weren't tons of rock inhibiting the signal. What we've done is use the automated tour guide system installed throughout the cavern. With a little creative rewiring, it allows us to communicate straight to the Big Room." Again the Colonel looked puzzled. "The Big Room is a cavern adjacent to the one the lunchroom is in."

"All right, you mean I can give an order on this walkie-talkie; a park ranger repeats it on that radio controlled tour guide do-hickey, and they can hear my order seven hundred-fifty feet below me?"

"That's exactly what I mean."

"That's some ingenious thinking. You did much better than I first thought. I'm going to get my troops started moving through the cave. Let's put a guide with each team of ten soldiers. We'll secure the caverns all the way from the lunchroom to the mouth of the cave. Any injured or lost tourist will eventually run into one of our teams and we can lead them to safety. And, with your help, I can command everything from here."

In moments his troops began coordinating their efforts with the park rangers. They went to work immediately ensuring the safety of the escaping guests. Some had indeed injured themselves cutting corners and trying to run straight up the switch-backed paths. Others, panicking in an effort to escape to the surface, found themselves lost.

Park Ranger Ron called in a number of professional spelunkers acquainted with the cave's layout to help methodically search for lost individuals. Soon all of the park's registered guests were accounted for, as either a hostage or one of the more fortunate who made it safely out of the cave. Eventually, the identity of the hostages would be extrapolated and made available to the leaders of the law enforcement organizations.

Working together, the military and the park rangers, secured the natural entrance of the cave and the *Big Room*, posting sentries for surveillance and intelligence gathering as close to the underground café as possible. The Colonel ordered a methodical invasion as if the cave were a military compound to be infiltrated.

On the far side of the *Big Room*, a few tourists found themselves trapped, unable to leave without passing through this no-go-zone. Luckily, a park ranger was there with them, attempting to keep them calm. Those paths were diligently monitored, not because they thought a tourist would dare run for safety, but rather because the Colonel ordered a shoot on-site command for the terrorists. If they dared leave the lunchroom, they were dead men.

In a preemptive measure, a call went out for any off duty medical staff to help with an unidentified crisis at the caverns. Having no idea what they were volunteering for, doctors and nurses from as far away as Las Cruces began pouring in. Once they arrived, the park rangers quickly apprised the newly assembled medical team of the hundred hostages. Soon an emergency medical triage station was located in a large tent placed squarely in the middle of the parking lot of the *Guest Information Center*. It quickly became a fully functional hospital. They hurriedly prepared for the worst, and possibly for the inevitable.

Inside the information center, Agent Keller barked her orders, "We have names for these guys. The mouthy one told the guard, who they released, exactly who his buddies are."

Agent Hinez said, "That's extremely odd. Usually, a team as efficient as these guys doesn't give up information leading to their identity."

"It's like he's giving them up to us, or something." Keller demanded, "Whatever his reason, I want to know everything about them. Do they have any other weapons except the miniature cannons the guard says they're carrying? Are they married? Where do they live? What did they have for lunch today? I want to know everything."

Her team snapped to obey her orders.

To ranger Ron, Keller said, "You've been talking to these guys. They know your voice. I want you to introduce me to them." She handed him back the microphone.

Over the intercom, the voice clearly identifiable as the ranger Ron said, "Mr. Terrorist. There's someone here who wants to talk to you."

"This is FBI Special Agent in charge, Charlene Keller. I'm going to take over the negotiations and parley for the U.S. Government in this arbitration. Who am I talking to?"

Harvard had been toying with the park ranger. Even though the man had been doing his best, he was no match for Harvard's wit. He'd been waiting for the FBI negotiators. If he had ever been eloquent in his life this was the time for him to prove his skill. He had to stack his aces carefully, knowing when to play his cards, and it was time he played his second ace.

Harvard smiled arrogantly. "I'm a negotiator for the Native American Tribal Council; a liberator of the Native American People. I intend to expose the improper treatment of Native Americans by the government of the United States."

Agent Keller didn't quite get her finger off the talk key fast enough and Harvard heard "Holy shi—" before he was disconnected. He had successfully put her off her game.

By turning a hostage situation into a political statement he had changed the rules of the game. She couldn't approach this with usual by the book responses.

Before she thought through her response, the FBI negotiator returned saying, "Good try, but I'm not buying it. Political protests don't start by asking for four million dollars. You're out of your league here." She took a deep breath and asked, "What exactly are you talking about?"

"Just like the Alcatraz occupation of 71 and the occupation of Wounded Knee in 73, this is a protest by occupation."

"You're not serious. You can't protest on behalf of the Native American Tribes. Especially if you're not Native American. Let's put that aside and get down to you letting the hostages go."

"I'm sure those USPP officers delivered the names I gave them. Look them up and cross-reference them with the Native American registry. Then I'll talk terms. This is for real."

"I have fifty soldiers, thirty park rangers, and a dozen USPP officers here. There is no way to escape. Turn the hostages loose and let's get this over with."

"Lady, you have no idea who you're talking to. We are Native Americans registered with the tribal reservations, a sanctioned, and according to United States' law a sovereign nation. Just like the USA, we hold land and make laws."

"I know about reservations. You think talking about Native American rights makes you a big shot. Every school kid knows everything you've already said. This is nothing special."

"You want special. Lady, I'll give you special—holding a hundred helpless hostages makes this special."

"So, you're hiding behind the political skits of racial discrimination and pretending it makes felony Kidnapping justified?"

"FBI lady, you better listen and listen well. I have no intention of moving one inch until every demand I have is met. Get this through your thick headed erudite skull because I'm making it perfectly clear, the future welfare of a hundred helpless souls are in your hands. If you want to treat them with frivolous, and bureaucratically flippant disregard then there's going to be a lot of killing. So, are you ready to listen instead of running your mouth off?"

"Talk, I'm listening."

"Now, as ambassadors of the Nation of the American Natives, we are not accountable to the federal laws of the United States."

Agent Keller took her finger off the *talk key* on the microphone, and even though Harvard couldn't hear what she was saying she whispered to Agent Hinez. "Get me a lawyer who knows about this tribal law stuff he's spouting." Her team looked from one to another not sure what they were supposed to do. She looked sternly and added. "Take the chopper, and get a knowledgeable lawyer airlifted here immediately."

The colonel asked, "I'm just guessing, but this isn't the usual demands of a hijacker, is it?"

She answered him, her tone cool and aloof. "No, Colonel, it's not."

Harvard was still talking on the intercom. "I want to make a declaration of occ—"

"Mr. Indian guy. Take a break from declaring anything. I'm turning the intercom off and I'll get back to you later." She put the microphone by the intercom and turned to the Colonel. "Don't you have a job to do or is hovering over my shoulder your new life's goal?"

"The manual says never tell the hostage-taker no. You may have just killed the hostages," scolded the Colonel.

"Right now he's more interested in his own rhetoric than mine. It will take a minute to sink in that I'm really not listening to his ranting. Anyway, he's not going anywhere."

Harvard was yelling into the intercom mic trying to get someone's attention. She had turned the volume down to a whisper.

"Colonel you have one thing right. This is unacceptable." She turned and glared at the park ranger who had been trying to negotiate. "Why were we not informed of this before now?"

He replied, "I didn't know. This is the first he said anything about it. All he told me was they wanted four million and a helicopter ride to get away to a certain Native American Reservation," He looked down at his notes, "the Jicarilla Apache Indian Reservation north of Los Alamos."

The Colonel frowned. His mistrust of the woman grew exponentially. Political bureaucracy was never his strong point. He had always blasted his way in and patched up the egos of his superiors later. The colonel said, "Maybe your balls aren't as big as you thought. This guy put you in your place real fast. I don't think it a good idea to break communication with the terrorists."

"He'll still be there. Where the hell do you think he's going?"

"It's against the expected conduc—"

She interrupted. "Colonel with all respect, shut the hell up. Haven't you figured this guy out yet? He knows our usual strategy. He's ready for me if I go by the book. "

Harvard knew he had rattled her. He kept yelling into the microphone only to make her all the more agitated.

Mika said, "Boss, looks like they don't want to play your game. This is bad—right?"

"No, Mika. Everything is just fine. What choice do they have but to listen to our demands? This is just a small setback."

Harvard's men looked from one to the other. This part wasn't in their orientation. Hinto walked over to Tarby and asked, "What the hell is he talking about?"

Tarby shrugged. "I don't know, but ya have to admit he has style. I'm liking what he has to say." He looked over at Mika, and seeing the worry on his face, he replied, "We're in way over our heads. Harvard is the only one who can get us outta here now. We gotta trust him."

Hinto replied, "Something tells me we're not getting our million."

"Stay with the plan." Tarby urged. "It's the only way out of here."

Once again, Agent Keller reengaged the microphone. "So, you're telling me this action is sanctioned by *The Joint Council of Native American Tribes?*"

Harvard enunciated each word forcefully, "What I'm telling you is that this is *not* an act of terror, but an act of *protest* to inform the people of the United States about the gross mistreatment of the American Native People at the hands of the U.S. Government, past and present."

"You want to know what I think? I think you're full of shit. You're a bunch of cowboys from Texas who had more time than brains."

Harvard fell silent, literally dumbfounded by Agent Keller's resistance to hear his political babble. For the first time ever Harvey, Harvard, Parker was pushed into a corner and struck speechless. Agent Keller had accomplished something even Ruffio Souza with all his intimidating, musclebound minions couldn't do.

After walking in a circle—thinking, and not knowing what else to say he yelled, "Mika, pick out a lovely young woman from among the hostages. We'll shoot her first and send her body up the elevator as a present for the FBI lady."

Agent Keller could hear the hostages cry out and beg not to be chosen. "Just use Sailor Suzie there. She's been a good little girl so far." Mika pulled her to the front of the crowd and was pushing her to sit on the floor before Harvard. Donald yanked her from Mika's grasp, pulling her back, and sat in her place.

Harvard looked Donald in the eye and said, "It doesn't matter who. I just need a warm body to turn cold—dead cold." He put the guard's revolver against Donald's forehead and cocked the hammer. All the hostages cringed and yelled for him to stop.

Hearing the gasps of the captives, Keller turned the mic volume up to ten. On the intercom in the cavern, her voice was tinted with a metallic twang. "All right, all right... I'm here. I'm listening. I only hope you have something more interesting to say than the lies you've already told me."

Donald scurried back to Margret's side and Harvard turned to walk back to the intercom.

He said, "This is no lie. You better check it out for yourself." He cleared his throat and continued. "This is an act of protest by occupation. As a sovereign nation, the lands now owned by the Native American people, commonly called reservations, are a nation unto themselves. We have our own laws and police force." Harvard swallowed hard and pulled out his third ace. "We, as ambassadors of the Native

American Nation, hereby claim the right of sovereign immunity for this protest."

Neither her training nor her experience had prepared her for this. The person in charge of the terrorists wasn't a simpleton, some wild cowboy who had taken hostages on the spur-of-the-moment. He was knowledgeable, well-spoken, and savvy. It appeared he was well versed in the United States position toward indigenous tribal natives.

The Colonel sat in a modern looking metal-framed chair and grinning like the Cheshire cat. From the look of him she could tell without a doubt, he believed she would stumble and ask for his help. He had watched as she started out playing mental chess with this terrorist who turned the tables on her. She couldn't measure the colonel up—not by the look of him. From what she could tell, he wasn't sure if his faith in this self-sure lipstick wearing FBI agent was warranted. Her unorthodox method had turned the game from chess into Russian roulette. She was gambling with a hundred lives and he didn't feel good about it.

She had arrived ready to talk some money-grubbing criminal into giving himself up. She wasn't prepared for a well-planned political demonstration. But, why had the terrorists asked for money if their motivation was political? Something didn't add up.

"When are you sending the journalist down here for my interview?" He paused. "I'm waiting."

Agent Keller had a few cards of her own to play. "Give me time to make arrangements," Agent Keller pleaded. "I can't just reach Walter Cronkite by calling his phone. He has secretaries who have secretaries and publicity people who have people. Be patient."

"You're stalling, Agent Keller," Harvard said.

Agent Hinez tapped her on the shoulder. She clicked off the microphone again.

"I can put in a call to speak to the major networks. I'm sure one of them will want to do the interview."

She turned to her team and said, "Hell no. We can't put a journalist in there with him. Cancel all of those calls. If we get him in the same room with Dan Rather or Walter Cronkite, as persuasive as he is, he'll be elevated to the level of a freedom fighter—a martyr for a cause. I have no doubt he'd manage to sway the public in his favor, and I don't even want to think about where this could go from there."

He stated, "We have to tell the media something. They're about to break down the door of the guest center, hammering us for information."

"Okay, let me think."

The Colonel sat across the room, his smile transformed in to a glare when he said, "At midnight I move my troops, no matter what." He pulled a cigar from his pocket, and snipped the end, preparing it for smoking.

Agent Keller pointed to the sign hanging above the door's illuminated exit sign. "Colonel, can't you read. No smoking in this part of the facility." She smile back at the Colonel daring him to reply. Banter with McMillian was a distraction and she needed to concentrate on the situation at hand. It was her turn to make a move in whatever game she and the terrorist were playing.

She only struggled with her thoughts briefly before she decided. "Agent Hinez," she called out, "The guard said one of the men asked for something much less, right?"

Hinez answered, "Yes, let's see... It's on this official affidavit signed by the USPP officer in question." He gave the document to Agent Keller.

She took a moment to read the affidavit before saying, "All right then, write this down, this is the official press release. *Four armed men kidnapped the caverns at 3:30 pm. They demanded a million dollars and a plane to take them to Brazil.*" She smiled. "The public doesn't need to know more than that. Not right now anyway."

Agent Hinez turned and started toward the room where the press waited. Before he reached the door, Keller called to him, "Oh yes, the report also said one of the terrorists had a flask. Tell the press they're drunk. As a matter of fact, tell them the gunmen have offered to trade the hostages for a bottle of whiskey, but recanted when we didn't have any here onsite. About the hostages, tell them the majority of the captives are actually at the other end of the Big Room, safe and out of harm's way. They just can't get out because the gunmen are controlling the pathway out. Get that? Use the word captives, not hostages and no mention of the word protest either."

"Why? I mean, are you sure you want to tell the press lies?"

"I'm sure as hell not telling them the truth. We have to keep a handle on this situation, and it's not completely lying. It's misinformation for the good of all concerned."

Agent Hinez took notes in an effort to not forget anything Agent Keller had said.

She sighed and added, "And, when you talk to the press, paint these guys as rogue cowboys, just good old boys who's fun went a little bit too far." She smiled to herself. "Use verbiage to will make them sound less dangerous and stop any panic which might be generated by the thought of a terrorist attack happening on U.S. soil, and especially at a U.S. controlled facility."

"When you put it that way," Hinez replied, "it would make people lose faith in the government if they knew the facts, but what they don't know won't hurt them. And, lately, the government's been getting nothing but bad press. Starting with Watergate and the botched handling of the military exiting from the Vietnam Conflict, and President Carter still hasn't mopped up Nixon and Ford's mess. We seriously don't need any more bad press gumming up the governmental works. We need a win on this one."

Keller requested, "Get FBI Director Webster on the phone. I've got to talk to him, as soon as possible."

CHAPTER TWENTY-TWO

Agent Keller
July 10th, 1979
Tuesday
5:30 PM
The lunchroom of Carlsbad Caverns

Harvard was tired of the silence. After he stated his demands and gave his elaborate declaration, he expected some kind of pause, but it was taking too long. He should be getting a formal reply, a counter offer from the government limiting the demands he made. At least the negotiator should be begging for the release of more hostages.

Agent Keller didn't reply. In the cave, the hostage's loud murmurings and the soft high pitched hum of the florescent lights were louder than the intercom's crackling static. There could only be two possibilities for the silence; either Keller was frustrated and didn't know what reply to make or she talked to someone in Washington who backed down because of his political outcry and was willing to meet his terms. Whichever was true, Keller continued to give

Harvard nothing but dead air. Impatient for a reply he said, "Hey, FBI lady. Did you understand me? I'm not speaking to an imbecilic moron, am I?"

Agent Keller's reply was firm and commanding, "No, I understood every word. I was making arrangements for you."

He had her attention again. It was time to give her another dose of political propaganda. "Great, then hear this. We also declare every citizen of the Indian Nation is an ambassador to the USA and the land they own outside a reservation becomes an international embassy where only the laws upheld by the Tribal Councils of Native American People have legal jurisdiction. This is a rule of law in agreement with tribal treaty going back over a hundred years when my people took the Trail of Tears, and secluded themselves in the lands your government promised to us. In a racial act of criminal atrocity, the U.S. Government then broke that treaty by allowing the sale and ownership of those properties to non-native people."

He paused only long enough to breath. "We are hereby demanding recompense and stating a declaration: henceforth, this property, Carlsbad Caverns, is by law owned by The Native American People." He then repeated his demands to be sure she followed them to the letter. "After you deliver our four million dollars in small bills, we expect to be taken by helicopter to a sovereign native reservation where we will be outside the jurisdiction of the U.S. Government."

Harvard's lengthy speech had been well practiced and delivered at exactly the right time. The FBI indeed made a check of Mika and Hinto's nationality as recorded on their work applications. The box indicating they were Native Americans had been checked by each of the three known terrorists.

Keller whispered to Agent Hinez, "Where is my legal specialist? I don't have a clue how to talk him out of there if I don't understand his argument. Get the legal specialist here... now."

Pressing the button so Harvard could hear her again, she turned her attention back to the terrorists, "Assuming this is all true, I need a show of good faith to prove you won't kill the hostages before you're airlifted to the reservation."

Harvard, still one step ahead of her kept the hundred hostages in groups of twenty-five. He answered, "Certainly, I'll release twenty-five of them now. Send down the elevator. It had better be empty or there will be a lot of sad kiddoes tonight when they learn how your government screwed us Indians again and made us kill their parents as an act of war."

"Are you declaring war on the USA? Is that what this is?"

"I'm not declaring anything more than I've already said. Not unless you force our hand by putting agents in the elevator."

"Don't worry," she said. "We don't want bloodshed. We'll play nice."

Harvard warned, "Don't take this lightly, Agent Keller. This is not a game. We're deadly serious. If you want, I can shoot one hostage to prove it?"

"No! No, that will not be necessary. The elevator is already on its way and it's empty."

Tarby called Harvard over to where he held his hostages. "A woman is having a breakdown," Tarby said. "I ain't shittin' you, she's gone into some kind of serious nervous fit. She just keeled over and laid on the ground, gritting her teeth, and shaking. What the hell do you want me to do with her? I guess we scared her too bad or somethin'."

Harvard looked at him in disbelief. "Not now. Now when we're this close." Then he explained, "She's having an epileptic seizure. You did something to trigger it."

"Really, Boss man, I didn't touch her. She just fell down and started shakin'. What do I do now? I think she's dyin'."

"Your group will be the first to go topside. Take the men we had to rough up and put them in the elevator with her. We don't need them anymore. Be careful. Carry her as easily as you can into the elevator. All we need is for this to turn dark before we're ready." He turned to Hinto and said, "Don't let more than twenty-five go. Hear me. Only twenty-five."

Hinto smiled. He liked being put in charge. "Yes, boss. You can depend on me."

Under Hinto's supervision, five people filed into the elevator with both the epileptic woman and the battered men for the first trip to the surface. Over the next few minutes, the elevator returned and made two more trips. As promised twenty-five people in all were released.

Keller felt good about the progress of the negotiations. This left seventy-five hostages still held by the gunman. Again, Donald and Margret weren't in the number who were released.

"As soon as our helicopter is here," Harvard said, "let me know and I'll be ready to negotiate a few more releases."

She turned to her team, "That sounds promising. He's already planning on releasing more hostages."

The Colonel chuckled, "He's playing you like a fiddle. What needs to happen is for my team to charge in and take them by force. Terrorists only respond to one thing, brute force."

"In my experience when people get shot at they shoot back." She smiled. "Colonel that would... How did you put it? Have dead civilians lined up between here and the surface. You're proposing a flawed tactic. Friendly fire would kill half of the hostages before the terrorists surrendered. Yes, he thinks he's playing me. This one is smart. He knew exactly what we were going to do and what we expected him to say. For right now, he's putting the ball at our feet and daring us to kick it."

"What? If you're not going to take them by force then your only option is to give them what they want." The Colonel looked sideways at her. "Agent Keller, you gotta remember he's playing for keeps. Tell him we have a helicopter and he can get away to his reservation right now. Maybe then he'll leave and we can secure the cave." The Colonel chewed his words as he sometimes did. "You know this is all on your head. He starts shooting and the shit'll fall faster than a Corvette at Monty Carlo."

Ignoring the pressure the Colonel added to the already overtaxing situation, Keller prudently replied, "The only choppers we have are the Black Hawks."

"I know that. You sent the FBI bird away after some highfalutin lawyer, and the pompous jackass isn't here yet. But, we can use one of the military choppers that brought us in and finish this once and for all."

"I don't think they will give up their occupation even if we offered them a cruise ship and the crew to sail her. I think it's all about the four million dollars. Anyway, right now you can't. I don't know a lot about this Indian Nations stuff, but I do know it's illegal to send a military airship of any kind into the airspace of any sovereign nation without consent by the nation in question."

She chuckled back at the Colonel. "I'm not telling you anything you don't already know. You probably have the laws covering military invasion memorized. We have to not rush into anything."

She took a deep breath. "Breathe Colonel. Then set back and watch. I'm going to play his game better than he does. Right now this is a staring contest. We need to be quiet and give him a few minutes to feel rewarded for letting those hostages go. Anyway, even if we could use your Blackhawk, I'd rather get a plain chopper for Mr. Native American and his buddies. Not that they will ever get to it—not if we're lucky."

Then she spoke to the Colonel in a commanding tone. "All we need is for them to take command of one of your

Black Hawks out there. For all we know, this nutcase might change his mind and actually declare war on the US. Their firepower alone would put everyone in Carlsbad in harm's way."

Agent Hinez interjected, "Agent Keller, we can have another FBI chopper here in fifteen minutes."

She turned back to the mic and said, "Mr. Native American, whoever you are, we have a helicopter on its way. It should be here in about fifteen minutes. Are you satisfied with our arrangements?"

"Yes. You're learning, Agent Keller. If you want me to release hostages you listen and obey. I'm on top of this."

"And, I bet you like being on top. Isn't that right, Harvard?"

"Shut up lady. You're trying to distract me and I'm not falling for it. What would you know about it anyway?"

He paused waiting for her to answer. She didn't. He couldn't see her smile.

After a few minutes he said, "I'm releasing another twenty-five hostages now."

Mika led his group of hostages to stand in line at the elevator. They obeyed quietly waiting their turn for freedom. When the elevator doors opened they entered the car, filing in calmly, twelve in the first trip and thirteen in the second. The entire twenty-five left in an orderly manner without running or shoving—they were all at gunpoint, but still, no one panicked.

Only fifty hostages were left including Margret and Donald.

In a pleasant voice, Special Agent Keller said, "By the way... I can't keep calling you Mr. Native American. What should I call you?"

He responded, "Call me, Harvard."

"Like the college? Don't you think that's a bit vain? I mean, seriously, naming yourself after the university you attended." She was fishing for some information with which to identify him.

"Whatever you think, lady. Now, shut the hell up. When you have my four million dollars, we'll talk again."

*   *   *

Agent Keller let Harvard wait longer than she promised in hopes he would become anxious and make a mistake. She could have gotten on the intercom and eased his mind about the wait but she wanted him to stew his conscience, weighing out what he got this men into. She wanted him to feel the weight of his own dilemma. She was sure he would contact her next. She was wrong.

Harvard waited comfortably in the cave.

"Hinto, I'm hungry," Tarby said. "Go make us some cold cut sans."

"There are some already made in my serving bin," Hinto replied. "You watch my group and I'll get us some." In only a few moments he returned and handed Tarby a sandwich. He sat down next to Margret and Donald and began munching.

With her fears already baptized in tears, Margret found enough courage to talk. She whispered to Tarby, "You know how rude that is?"

He looked up surprised. "What? What's rude?"

"Eating, when we're all hungry."

"Margret don't talk to him," Donald said.

"It's okay," Tarby replied. "She's right, but there's nothing to do about it. You're a hostage, and according to Mr. Harvard, hostages don't eat."

She huffed. "I disagree. And, what about the restroom?" She bit her lip before she continued. "It's been a while. Several of the hostages have already wet themselves because they're afraid to ask for restroom privileges, and it's starting to stink in here. Will we get to use the facilities soon?"

"I don't know. I'll ask Harvard and see what he says." Chewing the last of his sandwich, Tarby stood and walked toward Harvard.

Only minutes later he returned. "Harvard said no. No trips to the facilities. He said everyone can shit their pants if they have to."

"I don't like shitting my pants. Would you?"

Tarby looked puzzled. "I guess not. But, I'm not a hostage. I don't have to."

"Stop talking to him," Donald insisted.

"I was only asking about the restroom."

"I don't care what you're asking him. It's going to lead to trouble." He pulled Margret closer to him. "As long as we're held hostage, they're terrorists. You can't just strike up a conversation like you know them."

"They are people and people can be reasoned with."

"Not some people. Trust me, I know."

*　　*　　*

It was thirty minutes later when Agent Hinez reported, "I just received confirmation the FBI helicopter has landed."

It only took moments for Agent Keller to relay the information to the terrorists.

"Great," Harvard said.

Mika yelled over to Harvard, "Boss, that's well and good but we're planting ourselves here until we get our money."

Harvard nodded. "You're right, of course. That's what you're here for, the money." He then spoke into the intercom. "Exactly what I wanted to hear, but we don't have the four million dollars. We're making camp down here until we get it." He paused for effect. There was no reply. He had to shake thing sup a bit. "If you wait too long, we start executing palefaces one at a time until we run out of warm bodies. If you want to turn over cold bodies to their families, you keep taking too long. Your stalling's going to get someone killed, get the lead out, FBI lady."

CHAPTER TWENTY-THREE

The Last Ace
July 10th, 1979
Tuesday
6:30 PM
The Guest Information Center

It had been three hours since the terrorists took control of the cavern, but for Donald and Margret it seemed like an eternity.

In the Command Center the FBI set up inside the building, Special Agent Keller was talking to her team when she said, "Okay, all is good. He thinks the helicopter has been here for an hour already."

The Colonel asked, "So, why hasn't he made any move toward it?"

"He's waiting on his money. He won't go anywhere without the money. I'm betting the reservation stuff was a bluff."

"You can't know that for sure."

"No, and that's certainly why I'm taking no chances." She turned to her team. "Where is my lawyer? Is it really so hard to find someone versed in American Native law?"

Hinez answered, "Well, it seems that it is. No one is claiming the expertise we need on this." He paused. "The good news is, they have the four million in small bills waiting in the chopper. The guys in Washington aren't messing with this Native American angle they're playing at. They want this over fast. The boys on the hill are willing to give them whatever they want."

"Damn," blurted Agent Keller. "It looks as if the bad guys are going to get away with it this time." She looked up at Agent Hinez, and shouted in his face, "Do whatever you need to but get me a legal expert. I want to talk to someone about where I stand legally on this before I start making promises I can't keep, and people start dying."

Agent Hinez said, "I have a call being put in for Mr. Author Barnes, the Congressional Director of Native American Affairs. He advises President Carter himself. If anyone knows whether there's any truth to what this dirt-bag says, then it'll be him."

Keller huffed, "Time to get that son of a bitch back on the horn. He may not know it, but he's about to release more hostages." She spoke into the mic, "Harvard, are you there? I have your money."

"Great, send it down, and I'll let another twenty-five go."

"No, as always, you let them go, and then we'll send it down."

"Not this time, Sister. This time I don't feel so giving. We can argue about it, and I'll only release ten hostages and a dead one...or we can agree you'll send the money down, and I'll release the twenty-five as promised. It's up to you."

Special Agent Keller was trying every way possible to get the upper hand on the negotiations, but with the brass in Washington hurrying her and Harvard steadfast on his demands, she felt she had to give in.

She couldn't see him frown as he harshly said, "And, you better not try anything. The elevator better contain nothing but our money."

"No tricks. Here it comes. It appears you have a friend in Washington, Mr. Harvard. Someone who wants this ended quickly. The longer it continues the less patience your Washington supporter will have." The elevator went down to the lunchroom filled with four million dollars in a set of six large zipper bags.

When the money arrived Harvard allowed Hinto's group of twenty-five to exit up the elevator. This left only twenty-five terrified hostages held at gunpoint at the bottom of the caverns. As their luck persisted, Donald and Margret were in the remaining twenty-five waiting to be released or executed.

The terrorists were excited about the arrival of the money. Donald and Margret watched the gunmen as they immediately took the zippered bags, and empty out the cash into four large black trash bags. One for each of them. They carefully looked for tracking devices. They found them sewn into the lining of the zippered bags. They put the bags on the elevator with the last of Hinto's group who were exiting to the surface.

Harvard demanded, "How about my Journalist? I want someone I recognize."

Special Agent Keller said, "How about a news reporter from a local television station? Would you recognize Nathan Canterbury? He's on television every day, surely you watch the news?"

It was evident for the first time Harvard wasn't in charge of the situation as he wanted to be. "I was looking for someone more in Barbara Walter's league. Not some country-bumpkin desk anchor from a local TV station."

Keller was silent as Harvard pondered his options. He had his money, and the helicopters were waiting. He could accept this small concession and go with it or he could wait and get his Barbara Walter's interview.

He conceded by saying, "Yes, I would recognize Mr. Nathan Canterbury." He was feeling the pressure. Time wasn't on his side anymore. The longer this held out the greater the chance some trigger happy jarhead would end up shooting one of them and then he would have to retaliate, or possibly Hinto would get pissed off and shoot one of the hostages. He hadn't planned on anyone actually dying. If his plan went off as it was supposed to, the FBI would simply take them to the reservation as he asked. Harvard conceded, "Okay. The news reporter for KQAP Channel 10 News will do. Is Mr. Canterbury there with you now?"

"No, but he'll be here in about ten minutes." She put her hand over the mic and said, "Take a chopper and get Canterbury here in ten minutes—the clock is ticking." She redirected back to the intercom. "Harvard, he'll be down as soon as he arrives."

"That's more like it." There was silence and then Harvard said, "Since you didn't get me, my famous journalist, you'll have to do me one more favor."

"Oh, and what's that?"

Keller still didn't know his plan, he had to make it sound as if his concession was spontaneous. It was time he played his last card—his last ace. "I know you won't be able to outright arrest us inside the reservation, but I have no doubt your government will immediately petition for extradition. I want all federal charges dropped for me and my three friends. We'll agree to plead guilty to a misdemeanor charge but not kidnapping or attempted murder."

She shook her head and said, "I can lie and tell you something to make you release the hostages, but you know, you just asked for the green cheese moon and a spoon to eat it with. I can't guarantee that, not in good faith. It's my opinion no judge will ever go for such a reduction in your charges. My God man, you kidnapped a hundred people. Took them captive at gunpoint, and caused irreparable damage to a national treasure. It would be like spanking your hand and letting you go." She hesitated before continuing. "Harvard, did you hear me?"

He whispered to himself, "No plan of operation extends with any certainty beyond the first contact against a hostile force."

He had planned from the beginning to play his last ace in a swap for a favor, he just hadn't known what he would be trading it for. He certainly didn't intend to exchange it for his world shattering interview—the interview with Barbara Walters would have made him a national hero.

His miscalculation was that he thought the negotiator would want to bargain with him more than she had. Instead of bartering she was contentious and hard to manipulate. In a way she reminded him of himself. She was perhaps the smartest woman he had ever met, and it took all his willpower to resist her occasional flirty demeanor.

Without being able to barter for some other part of his demands he had to concede to an interview with a local TV personality.

His thoughts raged. *Perhaps it won't make any difference. My story is so big, so front page, it couldn't matter if a local TV reporter or a New York desk anchor did the interview—the results should be the same. From here on in, I'm playing High-card with this she-negotiator. Every hand matters, but I have to play it out one card at a time. I'll have to ponder what she says every time before replying to her. She's smarter than the average negotiator and has a damned sexy voice too.*

Harvard said, "I tell you what I'll do. You send down the journalist and I'll release fifteen of the hostages. I'm keeping the last ten for the deal-breaker. If I don't get the reduced charges I might as well kill them in cold blood. Don't make me do that. You hear me FBI lady? It's up to you. It will be like you pulled the trigger on the last ten yourself? Send down the elevator now. I'm reminding you we'll have three Russian-made assault rifles trained on the elevator doors. If I see an agent or soldier they're as good as dead."

She said, "No problem. Mr. Canterbury will be here in a few minutes."

Hinez said, "As you anticipated they found the trackers and sent them back up with the hostages. If that money gets out of the cave then we have no way of knowing where it's going. We'll find it one bill at a time through its serial numbers."

"Right now I could care less about those trackers. I want these creeps. I certainly don't want them to get out of the cave with or without the money, but the Washington boy's club is giving them everything they ask for and putting the thumbscrews on me." She tilted her head forward and rubbed the back of her neck. She needed another angle, a crowbar of an angle, with which to work on these guys.

"Agent Hinez," called Keller, "is the press still here?"

Hinez laughed at her intensity, "Are you kidding? Like they're going anywhere till this is over." It was a response no other team organizer would give his team leader, but they had a repertoire, a history, making the team a close-knit and efficient machine. Still, he may have just crossed the line.

"You don't have to get sarcastic," she retorted. "What did our team dig up as far as personal weapons these dirt-bags own?"

"The sales records and the licensing bureau have Hawk, Thompson, and Loadstar down for two shotguns and a .22mm rifle. This Harvard character doesn't seem to even exist. It's probably a fake name." He paused reading from two different documents. "However, the officers who were first released said he had a revolver."

"Okay, take one of the lady members of the press to the lunch room the park rangers set up in the parking lot. Act casual and drop that information on her as if you slipped and it just came out. I think this Harvard is using those weapons as a ploy to distract us from other facts. I don't want the words *Russian Assault Rifles* anywhere in this story."

When Agent Hinez returned Mr. Canterbury had arrived and was waiting patiently in the lobby of the Guest Information Center. Keller said, "Mr. Canterbury, I'm sorry to keep you waiting."

Canterbury replied, "I was writing up the part of my story where I rode in one of the military's Black Hawks to get here. I can't wait to get started writing the real interview. It's a huge story. My name will be right up there with Carl Bernstein and Ed Bradley."

"I'm afraid you've been misinformed." She gave him an intense stare. "If you want this interview, you'll do exactly as I tell you and nothing more. You're to go down and take notes, but when you return to the surface, those notes will be destroyed because your story will be written for you by my team. All the content will be altered. You do understand, you were never going to actually write what the terrorist says." Canterbury could see Agent Hinez was already busy, working with what looked like two public relations specialists, writing the official version of the story.

"This is unethical. I protest. I have journalistic rights."

"Perhaps it is, and you do have certain rights. Just remember, Mr. Canterbury, I have the right to put you on a chopper right now and take you straight back to Carlsbad.

Unless you agree that no stinking terrorist's sob story is more important than the U.S. national pride, and the confidence the people of the United States have in their law enforcement you have wasted your time. If you can't make these concessions then there will be no interview."

Canterbury thought about what this interview would mean to his career. No one would know if he allowed Keller's team to write it for him. Could he afford to miss this golden opportunity? He asked, "This would be something between just you and me. My employer won't ever know about it? If he learned of this deal I'd be finished as a news reporter. Even the implication of this kind of fraud and my career would be done for."

"Not only am I handing you a career-making story, but I'm offering you an incentive." She wrote on a piece of paper, laid it on the table, and pushed it over to him. "I'll give you credit for the entire negotiations and a bonus. I wrote a dollar amount on that paper. Is it a deal?

He picked up the folded paper and read what she had written. He whistled.

"Well, sir. What's your decision?"

He stood in silence.

"Agent Hinez, please escort Mr. Can—"

"I'll do it."

"I'm sorry. What?"

"I agree, the terrorist story isn't what's important. In this case, it's the fact that I'll be telling the story." He paused thinking about his decision. "Yes, that's the important thing.

Someone's going to get the flash and glamor from this interview and it might as well be me."

She looked him straight in the eyes and said, "You realize, no one can ever know about our deal, and you'll never be allowed to tell any other version of this as long as you live." He just sat there staring at her, so she repeated herself. "You know what you're signing, don't you?"

After a few minutes, he nodded and said, "I understand. What your team writes is exactly what he says and what I will see."

"Fine. Agent Hinez, get the security documents for Mr. Canterbury to sign." Keller smiled. "If you ever breach the contract you've made with the government of the United States, you will forfeit not only your right to freedom but also your U.S. citizenship." She leaned toward him and roughly said, "Remember, break your silence, and we'll put you in a hole so deep, it'll make the caverns pale in comparison." After Canterbury signed the documents, she collected the papers, smiled and handed them back to Agent Hinez.

She turned to the intercom and pressed the talk key. "I'm sending your journalist down in the elevator."

MIDDAY'S STARLESS MIDNIGHT

CHAPTER TWENTY-FOUR

Leaving Donald
July 10th, 1979
Tuesday
7:28 PM
The Lunchroom at Carlsbad Caverns

In the next twenty minutes, as promised fifteen more hostages were ushered out of the elevator back to freedom. Margret had been chosen as one of these fifteen, but Donald wasn't so lucky.

Before Harvard released her, Margret argued with Donald. "I can't leave you here." Turning to Harvard she pleaded, "You have to let him come to the surface with me." Harvard stood in silence as they pushed her toward the elevator. "What will I do without him?" She shrieked as the elevator doors closed behind her.

Donald didn't reach out for her or open his mouth to say a word. He simply sat behind Harvard, serene and completely composed. With a silent thankful prayer he watching his bride being loaded into the steel box and lifted to freedom.

*   *   *

Agent Hinez rushed into the Command Center. "Agent Keller, you have a phone call."

"I don't have time for phone calls unless it's an Indian lawyer with some really good news."

"No. It's Director Webster."

"Did you bring him up to speed?"

"Yes, but there's a hitch."

She snatched off her earring and pressing the phone receiver to her ear answered the phone. The conversation was short and to the point with Agent Keller saying, "I see," and later, "If that's what congress wants." The conversation ended with an abrupt, "Yes sir."

"What was that all about?" Agent Hinez asked.

"More pressure for Washington. This is making things get hot on the hill. Webster was only delivering their message."

"And, what was the message?"

"Settle this thing without fanfare as quick as possible, and do it anyway I can." She rubbed her neck. The stress was building up and making her entire back cramp. She stated, "Same song and dance as before only the director was more emphatic this time. He thinks I'm sitting on my hands. The command was, 'Do it faster.' Congress doesn't understand the logistics of a negotiation like this. Fast means dead bodies and I'm not gambling with anyone's life."

The Colonel said, "That's the smartest thing you've said all day."

*   *   *

Donald watched Margret leave in the elevator. It was the first real lucky thing he could remember happening in his life. His sole prayer during the entire ordeal was for her to be safe, and at last she was. Once he was sure of her safety Donald spoke, "Harvard, that is your name right? At least that's what you keep telling people to call you."

Harvard turned, and for a moment, he was shocked to know one of the hostages was actually brave enough to talk directly to him, much less call him by name. "Yeah, what's it to you?"

"I was just thinking about your agenda here. I mean it never was about the money... not for you. As I see it the money was for your buddies. You have a different agenda, it's the Native American thing. Isn't it? I guess I'm confused by all the legal-sounding jargon you spouted off at the FBI Lady? Are you an activist or a terrorist?"

Harvard answered with silence. He didn't have to explain himself to anyone, especially one of the hostages.

Donald hesitated before he said, "It would make a great smokescreen. Well, if the press reports it. It could cause enough stink and smoke to cover your escape."

"I think you talk too much for a hostage. Didn't your mother teach you, silence is golden?"

"No, not really. I learned a different lesson. It's called, do unto others as you would have them do unto you. Maybe you'd like to be my hostage for a while and we could see what happens?"

Donald gave Harvard a sideways smile. This guy was almost as arrogant as he was.

"Yeah, you think? Like that's ever going to happen." Harvard laughed. "I think your mama should have told you about what happens when people talk too much. They get smacked around." He couldn't hide his grin. "For a skinny little pip-squeak, you got some brains in there. Kid, I like you. I hope I don't have to kill you." He reached down and felt of the wilting boutonnière pinned to Donald's shirt. "It'd be a shame to make your bride a widow so soon. Now, sit still and shut the hell up."

*   *   *

In the Guest Information Center, on the ground level, Margret stepped off the elevator. She was greeted by waiting military personnel who escorted her to the triage unit where she would be checked by the emergency medical staff. As they gave her a thorough physical exam, her every prayer, her entire being focused on her husband.

Donald had drawn the lucky straw, so to speak, he and his carnation was chosen by Harvard to remain a hostage in return for the final demand, reduced charges from felonies to misdemeanors.

CHAPTER TWENTY-FIVE

The Director of Native American Affairs
July 10th, 1979
Tuesday
8:30 PM
The Guest Information Center

The phone rang in the *Guest Information Center* and Special Agent Keller took the call she had been waiting on. To her surprise, the voice on the phone wasn't the voice of a stranger, but rather, it was Agent Hinez telling her, Mr. Author Barnes, the Congressional Director of Native American Affairs had arrived, and was asking for her.

After the customary pleasantries due his office. She was direct as she relayed the exact words Harvard had used in his speech. She said, "He was specific about wanting something called *Sovereign Immunity*. What is he talking about?"

Mr. Barnes said, "First off, let me be clear. I've talked to members of the Native American Council and they are unaware of this protest, however, that doesn't mean this protester doesn't have credibility. All he needs is for this to hit the big market media and he'll be an instant cult hero."

The Director Barnes wiped his forehead with his handkerchief before continuing, "As I see it, he has a case here. It's true the U.S. has broken almost every treaty made with the Native Americans at one time or another. In this day of public awareness when media coverage shines a spotlight on an issue it's more difficult to break treaties than before, but secluded on the reservations in the darkness of unawareness and just plain ignorance, it's done in small ways by many so-called Indian Agents— almost daily. When these infringements are made it's just not talked about. Today, in this situation with him asking to see a journalist and his political savvy... It's my opinion, if we don't honor his request to take him to a reservation we could be viewed as the bad guys here. This is a sticky state of affairs to be sure. If it's not handled just right there will be hell to pay."

Keller retorted, "I've been able to keep everything about his Native American connection out of the press."

"I know, I've been keeping up with the case via the news. We can muffle his voice, but you have a hundred witnesses who heard him make his real demands." Barnes despairingly shook his head. "Too many *ifs* for anyone to control. Sooner or later the word's going to get out. The public is savvy. They'll wonder why he was flown to an Indian Reservation instead of us hauling him to an airport somewhere." He shook his head. "No, you won't be able to contain this, not completely. People will ask too many questions."

Hinez handed her a clipboard. She quickly read over the official interview as written by her team, and gave Hinez a nod, before she put her clipboard on the table.

"Get me Director Webster on the line."

In only seconds she was talking to the Director of the FBI, informing him about what she and her team had accomplished thus far.

"Director Webster, I've even made a deal with the journalist to alter his story. Just as congress requested, no fanfare. The public will be completely unaware of Harvard's actual agenda."

There was a silence in the Command Center as Keller listen to Director Webster.

"Yes sir. I have Director Barnes here at this time."

Again a silence, every time she stopped talking everyone in the room waited with heightened expectation for her next words.

"I have no doubt what's printed or reported in the media at a later time will be of little consequence. This event will blow over and disappear in the clutter of other news stories. One thing we can always count on is that Americans are always looking for the next big thing. Soon all this drama will be yesterday's news."

Another silence.

The pressure was high and she couldn't afford to lose the last four hostages because of some foul-up. She replied to Director Webster. "Alright. With congress' approval I'll move forward."

She hung up the phone.

She addressed the Colonel who was sitting in the same chair as before and smoking his cigar, ignoring the signage above the doors. She said, "I think I can get all the hostages out of there tonight if you'll work with me." His eyebrows went up as he blew out a long breath of smoke.

His reply was, "Whatever you need, Agent Keller. Whatever you need."

Returning to her conversation with Author Barnes, Keller asked, "So, Director Barnes, is it true, once he's there at the reservation, we can't touch him?"

The Colonel interrupted, "We could storm onto the reservation and take him along with his cohorts, by force."

"I'm sure you could, but it wouldn't be legal," Director Barnes explained. "It's true the Native Americans have been told they are a separate sovereign nation. A nation within a nation you might say. Even so, he's way out in left field by claiming the caverns for the Indians. The answer to that is unequivocally no. We're not giving the caverns to the Indian Nation. And yes, the son of a bitch kidnapped a hundred people, but even considering all his crimes, dominant public opinion can be swayed against us in this. We could easily look like the oppressors because of our past sins."

Keller looked puzzled. "What do you mean *dominant public opinion*? Like when the confederate flag's being defaced by the public, even when it's carved into veteran's headstones, and on national statues? I hear no charges are being filed against those perpetrators because they're crying how our forefathers were racial bastards?"

"Exactly," Barnes said. "Past sins can catch up with the nation and there is nothing we can do to stop the flow of public opinion. I think some of those protestors you mention were charged, but it's going to be hard to stop the trend. I'm no prophet, but someday the protestors may just tear down confederate statues, and the U.S. government will just set back and watch, doing nothing."

"So, what should I do about these so-called protesters at the bottom of the cave?"

"I recommend you do whatever you have to do to get those hostages out of there tonight. Make any promise you have to, and give them whatever it is they want, I'll back you up." He cleared his throat and added. "I heard what you told Webster on the phone, and I disagree. This is going to be too big to keep under wraps."

"Director Barnes," Keller smiled as she said, "the FBI has a damned big wrapper. Wait and see. I'm right about this."

*   *   *

It was only thirty minutes later when Harvard called for the elevator again. When the door opened this time at ground level, Mr. Canterbury stepped out into the command center followed by six more released hostages. Agent Hinez collected his note pad and ran it through a paper shredder. Only four hostages remained. Donald was one of the four who remained.

Harvard was on the intercom. "Hey FBI lady. You listening?"

Special Agent Keller answered, "Yes. I'm listening. What is it now?"

"All that's left is for us to get our reduced sentences, set these last few free, and get out of Dodge."

"You're supposing I've gotten approval to do that."

"All I need is your personal guarantee."

She said, "I've been speaking to the Congressional Director of Native American Affairs, and he has given the okay on your requests."

"All of them? Are they granting all my requests?"

"Yes, all of them. The helicopter ride to the reservation, and the reduced charges too. All approved by an official with more clout than I have."

"About time."

Keller said, "Right now, I'm more concerned about you. I don't want them to shoot you after all the effort I've gone through. You know the military is here ready to storm in and shoot you on-site."

"Agent Keller, you sound as if you care about me. Have I turned you to my cause?" There was a moment of silence before he said, "Tell me they don't make you wear one of those man suits."

"Yes, I wear a suit. Not a man's suit, but a suit."

"I bet you're a tiger in the sack."

"Harvard, don't be crude. I was only concerned because I value human life. I don't want anyone killed today."

"Tell me you didn't feel the magic between us. I'm sure you did."

"Harvard, you know what's between us right now? Three hundred tons of solid rock. That's what's between us."

"Right now I'm thinking more about satin sheets than rocks."

"That's not thinking it daydreaming, and from my point of view it's a nightmare."

"Ouch, you just popped my bubble."

"Believe it or not, all evening I've been working hard to get you out of that pit in one piece."

He looked at the scrawny man with a wedding boutonnière pinned to his shirt collar. "FBI lady don't worry about me. Worry about these pitiful palefaces down here. I still have time to clock one. Just tell me if you're going to support me in my protest?"

She laughed at him saying, "I can't support you in your protest, but you knew that already. You're no fool, Mr. Harvard. The single thing the government is standing firm on is their insistence about the Caverns being U.S. property. You must have known there's no way the U.S. was ever going to give these caverns to the Tribal Council."

He laughed. "That wasn't wishful thinking. That was strategy." He paused for effect. "I had to give those pencil pushers in Washington something to win on. Now, are you sure about those charges?"

Keller said, "Yes. I'm sure. You have my personal promise, based on what the Congressional Director of Native

American Affairs has told me. The charges will be reduced to misdemeanor charges. No Federal charges will be made."

"Great. Oh, we'll set these last four free after we get safely to the reservation. They will be accompanying us on the flight. You didn't think I was stupid enough to take your word about letting us go after we released all our hostages?"

Harvard shot a glance over at Donald and his three fellow hostages sitting on the line Harvard shot in the floor.

Keller replied, "I expected that." She clicked the mic off and turning to Hinez she said, "Keep the press in the annex building. Put guards at the door if you have to. I don't want them watching as Harvard makes his exit." She thought for a moment before turning back to the intercom and asking, "Will you allow the helicopter pilot to bring them back after he drops you off?"

"Certainly. I bet they'll be home in time to sleep in their own beds tonight."

Harvard dropped the mic and lifted his gun. He looked back over to the skinny guy with the boutonnière pinned to his printed satin shirt. "So, you're a newlywed and that's why you're wearing a dumb flower?"

Donald answered, "Yes, as if it matters at all. Why are you even talking to me? Just a few minutes ago you were telling me how my mama should have taught me to shut up and keep quiet."

"Yeah, I guess that's right. But, we're about to get to know each other a lot better. You're going with me to the reservation as my shield to protect me from the FBI snipers."

"You don't trust them to tell you the truth?"

"Oh yeah. They're telling the truth about the charges and taking us to the reservation, but they didn't say anything about firing on us when we get out of the elevator."

"Great. I get it. I stand in front of you and if they shoot, they shoot me first."

"Yeah. That's about the size of it." He looked the skinny man up and down. "What's your name kid?"

"It's Donald... and, I ain't a kid."

"No, and you're not much of a shield either. You're so skinny they might be able to shoot me and miss you altogether."

"Great. I'm not only a shield for a freaking terrorist, I'm a bad shield. I'm being ridiculed for being physically inappropriate for the task you're forcing me to help you with." Donald paused. Shook his head and said, "If I'm unfit to be your shield why choose me? You have my permission to use someone else."

Harvard laughed and said, "As it happens my pickings have dwindled to almost nothing and there's one thing you have, I don't know if these other guys have."

"What's that?"

He slapped Donald hard on the back. "A new bride, that's what. It'll play in the media better than if I were to choose just some old guy."

"You sure are into all the publicity stuff. I was listening to you talk to the news reporter about your cause." Donald looked over at Harvard's three accomplices. "Do you really believe in the things you told him? I mean the speech you gave him about Native American rights and all, it was pretty touching. Is that why you did all this?"

"Kid, I never do anything without a reason. It may not be the reason they see upfront, but there's a reason."

"I guess I was asking because, it's obvious to me, you're genuinely a smart guy. Have you ever heard about a guy by the name of Martin Luther King Junior? His thing was protesting, but he never used violence. He used passive aggression, with an emphasis on passive, to get his message out." Donald gave Harvard a sarcastic smile. "All you'll be remembered for is violence and terrorism." He leaned closer to Harvard and continued, "You had to know from the start you'd never get away with this. Seriously, what were you thinking? A smart guy like you should know better than to take hostages underground where there's only one safe way out, and knowing the firepower they have waiting up there. Even if they take you to a reservation do you think the Natives will protect you? They'll turn you over to the U.S. government with a ribbon on top."

Harvard swung his gun around leveling it on Donald along with a truckload of intimidation. "Yep, your right. The obvious wasn't it at all, not for me anyway. You see, I couldn't remain passive when I have so much to say. I had to make a stand that would make a difference." He pulled a cigar from his shirt pocket, lit it, and blew a long thin stream of smoke over Donald's head. "Mr. Donald Newlywed, do you think I made a difference."

Donald shrugged, "I may be wrong, and it seems I'm wrong a lot lately, but I don't think you can make something right by doing wrong. Usually I'm a passive guy. I know a thing or two about turning the other cheek." He looked Harvard in the eyes. "I don't think you've ever been passive one day in your life."

"Mr. Honeymoon, don't make me angry. You'll regret it."

"No. It's time for me to say whatever I want to. You can't kill me now. I'm your shield remember. You gave away all your other hostages. I'm all you have."

"Don't test me, kid. Even if I like you, there's no rule that says I have to turn you over to the FBI unbroken."

"Whatever you say, Mr. Harvard, sir. But, I don't think anything you said here is going to matter, not in the long run. All everyone will see is the brutality—the crime. These government types will find a way to cover-up your protest, and do whatever it takes to sweep the whole thing under the rug." He snickered. "It wouldn't surprise me if the official word about your demands was what the other guy said to the first guard who went up."

"What? You mean what Hinto said about wanting a million dollars and an airplane to Brazil?" He chuckled. "Don't make me laugh." Then he pressed his lips into a frown and said, "You really think they'd screw me over like that and hide my world-changing remarks?"

Donald wiped the sweat off his face with his sleeve and thoughtfully replied, "I work for a printing company. I mind my own business and do my job well. I've seen lots of guys who run printing presses just like mine. They get old and retire. Another guy, like me, comes in and takes their place.

It's the status quo. Everything working the same all the time every day. It's reliable and steady. When someone comes in and starts making waves over the newest thing, like some technology they've read about. It gets things all out of sync."

"What the hell are you telling me about printing presses for? I asked you a simple question."

"Because the government system is like my workplace. They like the status quo. And, today you shook things up pretty bad. I think they're going to do what they have to so that the status quo gets back to normal. Even if it means contradicting the media or even buying them off. And, especially if it means not giving the public the truth about your demands, then yes. Of course, it's only my option."

He spit. "Then all this will be for nothing."

"Maybe, but it's hard to keep a hundred witnesses from telling their experience about being held captive in the bottom of Carlsbad Caverns." He sighed. "Sounds like a fish tale or something a grandfather would tell his grandkids."

"Hell! You're right. If those hostages talk about my cause then the FBI will claim they're affected by Stockholm syndrome. Isn't that what they said about Sharon Tate? She sided with her kidnappers because of some psychological trauma?"

"Well, I can't say I haven't been traumatized. It's true. I'm just glad my Margret was one of the lucky ones you set free." Donald looked Harvard in the eyes, they were green. He had never noticed before. "Purpose or no purpose... Cause or no cause... You know if I get the chance I'll shove that fancy gun up your ass, and get away—I will"

Harvard frowned and said, "Stand up smart mouth. Hands together out front where I can see them." He took a zip tie and bound Donald's hands with it. "Have you ever been used as a human punching bag?"

"I bet I've taken worse from far better."

"I doubt it. Remember I don't have to let you go in like-new condition. I'm gonna break you up, little man."

With that said, he drew back and boxed Donald with a backhanded fist across the face. Donald let the blow spin him around. Using his momentum and his bound hands as a club, he swung hard, plowing into Harvard's ear and scraping the zip tie across his face—knocking Harvard to the ground.

Anger like Harvard had never known rushed over him. His fury overwhelmed him to the point that something inside snapped. It was like Harvard's entire universe suddenly tilted. His easy-going arrogance was transformed into primal uncontrollable fury. It flared in Harvard's eyes as the gangster turned terrorist, rubbed the back of his hand across his mouth. As he wiped his face, a streak of blood transferred from his lip onto the back of his hand. "You just bought yourself a ticket to sing with the angels." He leveled his rifle at Donald.

Hinto grabbed his arm and said, "Boss, if you meant what you said about the cause then messing this guy up will look awfully bad."

Harvard demanded, "Get out of my fucking way."

Mika joined in Hinto's plea. "We can't take a chance on that right now," Mika begged. "Your plan worked. They're offern' us a ride out of here. Let's take it."

Harvard knew they were right but his self-control was at a low ebb. He physically shook as he said, "You're right, but there's something about this guy. He makes me sick." He looked Donald in the eyes. "Someone needs to teach him a lesson. He's got a smart mouth, and he doesn't scare easily." Without hesitation, he slapped Donald's jaw with the butt of the gun. For the first time in his life, Donald saw the outcome of something turn better than the events that started it. In this case, he was certainly fortunate the butt of the gun glanced off his cheek without breaking his jaw. Harvard looked surprised when he didn't fall to the ground. Donald just spat blood to the floor and stared defiantly at Harvard.

Either Harvard was backing down, or he had just changed his mind. Then again, just maybe, it was Donald's luck.

"I don't have time for this shit." Harvard scoffed and announced, "Men, it's time to take a helicopter ride."

Harvard was all but dragging Donald along as the four gunmen stepped out of the elevator into the Guest Information Center. They expected to be facing a room full of military soldiers and FBI agents, all with their rifles leveled on them. To their surprise, the visitor center was empty except for Agent Keller and Colonel McMillian. They were unarmed and wanted to make a final deal.

The terrorists were silent as they held their hostages in front of them and pointed the guns at the Colonel and Agent Keller. If the terrorists intended on keeping their human shields close enough to be effective then the rifles proved to be a little too long to aim at the hostages. They weren't designed for such a close encounter. So, with them slung over one shoulder they had reverted to using the pistols taken from the guards. The inexperienced terrorists looked to Harvard for leadership. He was clearly in charge, and the others were way over their heads. If Harvard couldn't get them out of this no one could.

Harvard asked, "Are you the FBI Lady I've been talking to on the intercom?"

"Yes, I am. I'm Agent Keller and this is Colonel Henry McMillian of the US armed forces. We want to assure you, neither the military nor the FBI will interfere with you leaving the park. All we ask is for you to take me and the Colonel with you to the reservation. Of course, if you have us then you don't need two of these brave people you're holding as shields."

"This sounds like a trap. I let go of Honeymoon here, and one of those sharpshooters puts a bullet in my head."

"No tricks," The Colonel said, "We only want you to release as many of the hostages as possible."

Harvard turned sideways and gave his crew instructions. "I'm going to let go of Honeymoon and if they shoot me... you two fill these shits full of lead." He moved forward into position in front of the others. "Don't hesitate. You see blood start shooting."

Slowly Harvard let go of Donald and pushed him aside. Agent Keller walked calmly over to stand in front of him and put her hands behind her back. Harvard reached in his pocket for another zip tie. He waved it at the Colonel "I only have one more zip tie, so, we'll only be taking the FBI Lady."

Agent Keller said, "I can help if you'll allow me to." She was reaching slowly into her back pocket and brought out a pair of handcuffs. Harvard snatched them from her and cuffed her hands behind her back. Then it was Mika's turn. He released his hostage and the Colonel graciously walked over and took his place. Mika strapped Harvard's zip tie around the Colonel's wrists. Donald couldn't believe his luck. He wouldn't be making the trip to the Indian reservation after all. He was, believe it or not, being released. He had felt sure his curse of bad luck would make certain he was the very last one set free. He and the other released hostage ran from the building toward the soldiers who were standing calmly by the asphalt tour trail. They escorted them to the triage tent.

The four hostages and the four gunmen walked to the waiting helicopter. They were diligent to keep their human shields in front of them. Once inside the helicopter, Agent Keller said, "Harvard, don't you think it's about time to let the last two go?"

"I let them go and you two stay? Is that it? If I do, you can tell the judge I played by your rules and turned all the original hostages loose."

She answered, "Yes, it's a certified deal. Once there we vouch to the Tribal Council about your cooperation"

He glanced at his crew and said, "Sounds good to me."

He kept his pistol pointed at Agent Keller as the last two civilian hostages were set free.

Harvard asked, "Which reservation are you taking us to?"

Colonel McMillian replied, "We have notified the Mescalero Apache Reservation northeast of Alamogordo you're coming. I feel sure they have a welcoming committee waiting for you."

"That isn't the one I requested. I want to go to the Jicarilla Apache Reservation."

"We're aware of that, however, this is the closest one and the helicopter doesn't have enough fuel to make that trip. If you want to go now then it's the Mescalero Apache Reservation, or we wait for the chopper to go fuel up."

"Okay, Colonel. If you say it's the Mescalero Apache Reservation, then that's where we go. Sounds acceptable." He pointed the gun at Colonel McMillian. "Get this bird in the air. What are we waiting for?"

The pilot raised the collective control and the Helicopter lifted off the ground. Loaded with four million dollars, the terrorists, Agent Keller, and the Colonel in chopper they headed northwest.

Donald and the other released hostages tripped, ran, and staggered their way to where soldiers waited for them. They quickly cut their bonds and helped them past a line of military artillerymen with sniper rifles aimed at the terrorists. These were the men who were ready to take anyone of the hijackers down if they moved to harm either the Colonel or Agent Keller.

Before Donald entered the Triage Center he stopped and turned to look back at the helicopter as it left without him. He couldn't believe his luck. He thought he would be one of the four leaving with the terrorists.

The wind changed directions and blew a cool breeze toward Donald and the soldiers. An unexpected gust carried what could have been the only piece of trash in the parking lot onto Donald's sneaker. It was an ice-cream wrapper, one like they served in the subterranean café. It had blown out of a trash bin to plaster Donald's shoe with sticky ice cream residue.

"Man, how unlucky!" One of the soldiers said to the other. "Some nasty trash blew right at this guy's shoe like it had a guidance system or something."

The other soldier replied, "Yeah, glad it missed me."

Donald said, "It's okay. I'm used to it." He sighed and bent down to pick it off his shoe. Under the sticky wrapper was a hundred-dollar bill. Donald quickly stuffed it into his pocket and said, "Well, maybe my luck is changing." He breathed in. He could almost taste the difference in the air. He turned to feel a breeze blowing across the desert.

In a few minutes, the wind blew again. This time it blew across the gravel and concrete parking lot, and into the triage tent where Donald and Margret sat holding hands. Her eyes were dark because she had been crying and praying until she was hoarse. She held Donald close. "I can't believe it. I was sure they were going to kill you."

"I told you it was all going to be okay," he said.

Margret answered, "Yes. Yes, you did, and as always you were right Mr. Wiseman. You are always right." She paused and looked him in the eye. "I want to know what smart-mouthed thing you said to get yourself picked to be a human shield?" She rubbed her finger over the bruises on his face. "Looks like you picked a fight after I left."

He smiled sheepishly.

She exclaimed, "Oh hell's bells, you did. You picked a fight with the gunmen. You stupid fool. With your luck, you could have gotten yourself killed." For a brief moment she saw in his smile a glimmer of a rebel child she had never seen before.

There was laughter in his voice when he said, "No, Harvard wasn't going to kill me. I was a part of his plan ever since he saw this stupid flower on my shirt. He chose me because he figured out I was a newlywed."

"You picked a fight and it wasn't to defend me? Why Donald, That's not like you. You think he needed you but what if he had changed his mind at the last minute. He could have hid behind the other three men, using them as a shield."

"I think he planned this out and he was going to stick to the plan. You should have seen him. He wanted to kill me, but he knew if he killed a hostage his trip to the Indian Reservation would have been forfeited. No, they needed four human shields and there were only the four of us left—I knew they wouldn't kill me. And, anyway, it felt so good to bust that creep's lip."

"I can't take you anywhere, Donald Wiseman. Picking fights with men bigger than yourself, and with guns too."

"I can't believe it. You're worried about me beating up one of those terrorists."

"Oh, I'm not. I'm not worried about you. I'm worried about those other guys, those terrorists. I've seen you rush right at a man with a machine gun. Honey, you're the bravest man I've ever known."

He pulled her close. She wrapped her arms around him neck. "Next honeymoon we take, I think I'll show you how brave I am without the guns and the shooting?"

She looked him in his green eyes and said, "Sweetheart, You don't have anything to prove to me. I've known how brave you are all along. That's why I married you."

Donald only smiled at her.

"Oh, Donald. You're a genuine hero."

"I guess it took the whole tragic weekend for me to find out you feel that way." He started speaking in a pretentious English accent. Sounding like an English Lord, he said, "My Lady, maybe you should tell me these things so I don't have to face unsurmountable odds to win your favor."

Margret played along and replied, "Alright, Sir Donald of Carlsbad. Have no fear, my favor has been won."

Then in his usual Texas accent, he asked, "Can we go home now and have a calm uneventful life?"

"Yes. Yes, Mr. Wiseman, we can." She replied. "I have only one more thing to tell you." Donald looked up in quizzical apprehension. Then she continued, "Never take me to Carlsbad Caverns again as long as we live. For our second honeymoon let's go to Niagara Falls."

"Yes, Mrs. Wiseman. That's something I can do."

CHAPTER TWENTY-SIX

Resolution
July 10th – July 30th
Santa Fe, New Mexico

As promised Keller and Barnes accompanied the terrorists to the Mescalero Apache Reservation located between Carlsbad and Ruidoso. When they disembarked from the helicopter they surrendered their weapons to the Tribal Police who met them at the chopper. Taking no chances, their police had an arsenal of firepower leveled on the terrorists. Behind the police was a welcoming committee made up of *The Native American Tribal Councilmen.* The gunmen were taken into custody by the Tribal Police and jailed on reservation grounds awaiting an impromptu vote by the Tribal Council. The vote was unanimous. As expected the terrorists were sent back on the same helicopter they had arrived on, but this time they were held at gunpoint in the custody of the Tribal Police. They were flying to Santa Fe to stand trial.

In Santa Fe, The military bowed out of the situation gracefully, allowing the state to clash with the FBI. Federal authorities claimed that the terrorists could not be held by the state since their crimes took place at a federal facility, it was a federal matter. The State of New Mexico sued the U.S. Federal Government for custody of the terrorists, wanting to charge them with Felony kidnapping, attempted murder, and defacement of a state monument. The state lost the case and the terrorists were moved to Albuquerque. There the charges were reduced as Special Agent Keller had promised. The four pled guilty to misdemeanor charges of unlawful imprisonment and defacing public property. They were sentenced to one year without parole in federal prison. The official statement released by the FBI about the terrorist's demands was that the gunmen wanted a million dollars and an airplane to take them to Brazil.

As for Margret and Donald, when they arrived back in Lubbock, they went to Martha and Frank's house to return Frank's truck. Donald ignored his mother because she wanted to know what he had done to make the gunmen take everyone hostage. She was sure if Donald was involved then it had to be his fault.

Frank had not been able to convince the landlord to return the entire deposit, but he managed to get half of it back. He had also been lucky enough to find them a nice duplex apartment, *without bullet holes in the wall*, and it was only five blocks from where Donald's parents lived. Oddly after hearing his tale about confronting the terrorist, his brothers-in-law started treating him with more respect. Something had changed in the man Harvard had called Mr. Honeymoon. He couldn't remain passive when he had so much to say, and as a result, he distanced himself from his lifelong friends. He determined to make something of himself and those hoodlum friends would only weigh him down. They were family and he did see them once in a while, but only on occasion, even Margret had decided to only see her brothers on holidays.

Three years later, Donald and Margret found the perfect house to raise a family in. Oddly, several people had tried to buy it, but their offers had been rejected. When Donald applied it went straight through without a hitch. There they raised a family of their own.

Donald bought a single lottery ticket one afternoon in May of 85. It was a twenty million dollar winner. As it turned out, he won his millions of dollars the legal way. Everything in Donald and Margret's life wasn't always perfect, but what marriage is perfect. The thing they always looked back on was, if their marriage could withstand four terrorists holding them hostage under tons of rock then it could withstand anything.

Miss Sally was wrong about Margret's boobs. She was wealthy enough to afford a Hollywood plastic surgeon. They never drooped.

As for Harvard and his men, the turn key to their shortened prison term was that they could never divulge what actually happen in the cavern. Agent Keller explained in plain language saying if he ever told the true events he would be subject to felony charges. So, he took the agreement, signed the papers, and served his one year in prison. When he was released he was never quite the same. In fact he never went by Harvard again, from that day on he was just plain Harvey Parker.

The outlaws didn't want him back, and for the first time he didn't really belong anywhere or fit into society. He got his job back at the coffee shop and managed to scrap and save enough money to buy a new H.D. Electra Glide. It was the only thing people said he cared about.

Once he even got the nerve to call the news networks about his story. After putting in dozens of calls the answer was *don't call back*. No one wanted to listen to his version of the Carlsbad Occupation. They considered the whole thing ancient history.

After all, real news was happening every day. John Lennon had been shot while he was away. There were riots in Miami, and an oil profit tax was about to be passed that would make history. The hottest news in every headline was about a cancer like virus called AIDS which had been identified for the first time, and what news could compete with the first flight of Space Shuttle Columbia. He had a story no one wanted to talk about.

On a spring day in May of 1985, Harvey decided to take a ride out in the El Paso country side. The day was just a usual day until an eighteen wheeler passed him going no less than ninety miles an hour. The wind force around the fast moving truck pulled Harvey toward it. He overreacted and lost control. Harvey Parker died on that El Paso highway before emergency teams could reach him. They said if he had been wearing a helmet it might have made a difference, but he had always been too lucky to need one.

AUTHORS NOTE:

This is a fictionalized account of a historic event. I have a writer friend who in fact visited Carlsbad Caverns National Park the week of July 8th of 1979. Thankfully he was not one of the hostages taken in that historic event. He and his bride chose the caverns as their honeymoon destination, however, they didn't have as many misfortunes as Donald, and he doesn't have evil brothers-in-law.

Everything in my story is fiction except these facts: the terrorists owned two shotguns and a .22mm rifle; they asked for a million dollars and a plane ride to Brazil; they had a bottle of whiskey; they claimed to have set explosives along the paths to the lunchroom; they shot at the hostages feet, and one woman had an epileptic seizure during the tragedy. The gunmen did indeed discuss Native American rights, and they were given reduced sentences—spending only one year in prison.

These facts were published and are available to the public. Unlike my story, according to the media report at the time, most of the hostages were not in the lunchroom, but in a section of the caverns on the far side of the lunchroom and couldn't get out because the gunmen controlled the paths leading out.

This fictional account does not represent any actual person or people involved in the event. Outside of the fact, there were indeed four of the terrorists, all my characters—including the terrorists—are completely fictional. I created them to fit the fictional scenario I developed. I gave them fictional names, and romantically colorful lives, therefore, *The Outlaws* motorcycle gang, Harvard, Hinto, Mika, Tarby, Donald, Margret, and their families, Mr. Barnes, Agent Keller, the FBI team, the military Colonel, Director Webster, and the TV News reporter are all totally fictional, as well as, all the other characters. There is no truth in the events of this fictionalized drama about the 1979 terrorist attack on Carlsbad Caverns.

In Martian Luther King's acceptance speech for his Nobel Peace Prize, he used the term *Starless Midnight*. He used it in reference to the darkness of racism spreading over our land. In my story, the hostages were in a pit where the starlight couldn't reach them, and the cause Harvard so awkwardly and violently tried to bring to light was covered up, kept from the light of day, the night's stars, and the media. As gripping as his message could have been, it was only a fictional representation of actual facts.

Perhaps in my fictional world, Donald will someday make a statement for himself, not using violence but rather in his passive way. Violence may force people to change how they live, but it will never change humanity's heart. The only way people change is because they as a group have a personal epiphany—a new understanding of how we should live. When brothers, of all races and creeds, help brothers, and sisters help sisters to live together in harmony then and only then will we see Dr. King's dream come true.

As for the actual events, if the media reports of the *Carlsbad Incident* aren't accurate then only the FBI negotiator at the scene could possibly be the only person, outside of the terrorists themselves, who knows the truth. As for my version, remember, it's all fiction.

Made in the USA
Middletown, DE
11 March 2022